"What I Want In Life Has Changed Since I Left Texas,"

Maddie said again.

"What I want in life has changed, too, Maddie. We want different things, have different needs now than we did back then." He tilted her chin up and leaned close again. "All I know is that you should watch out, because I intend to cater to the part of you that still responds to me when we kiss."

"It's sheer foolishness that there are moments I can't resist you," she replied. His words made her heart pound, and now she was ensnared in his crystal-blue gaze. Panic gripped her. She was tumbling rapidly into a situation she'd hoped to avoid. There was the matter of their *daughter*— who he knew nothing about. "We're not going to rekindle what we had. We've both moved on and our lives have changed."

He ran his index finger down her cheek. "Some things haven't changed at all."

* * *

To find out more about Desire's upcoming books and to chat with authors and editors, become a fan of Harlequin Desire on Facebook www.facebook.com/HarlequinDesire or follow us on Twitter www.twitter.com/desireeditors!

Dear Reader,

Once again, I have set another book in Texas with its glittering, down-to-earth, friendly people and larger-than-life ways. This last story in my series about the handsome millionaires who have been friends since earliest childhood focuses on Gabriel Benton, Jake's younger brother. It is a story of reunion involving Gabe, the handsome blue-eyed rancher, and Madeline Halliday, a woman he has grown up knowing and once viewed as his best friend.

Their romance encompasses the triumph of love and forgiveness, qualities that belong in the deepest and longest-lasting relationships. I've said before that families are close to my heart and enter into the themes of my books, including this one. Family has a big influence on our lives, and that is true of Maddie and Gabe.

Friends and former lovers, the two encounter each other along a Texas highway. Gabe, a man accustomed to getting his way, cannot resist wanting to be with Maddie and talks her into dinner. He re-enters her life, stirring passion, guilt and—finally—the revelation of the secret that changes both their lives.

This book is a farewell to the four CEOs who all wear Stetsons, call Texas home and fall in love with exciting women.

Thank you for selecting my book.

Best wishes,

Sara Orwig

SARA ORWIG

WILD WESTERN NIGHTS

PLEASE RECYCLE · THIS PRODUCT IS RECYCLABLE

Recycling programs
for this product may
not exist in your area.

ISBN-13: 978-0-373-73123-7

WILD WESTERN NIGHTS

Copyright © 2011 by Sara Orwig

This edition published by arrangement with Harlequin Books S.A.

For questions and comments about the quality of this book please contact us at Customer_eCare@Harlequin.ca.

® and TM are trademarks of Harlequin Books S.A., used under license. Trademarks indicated with ® are registered in the United States Patent and Trademark Office, the Canadian Trade Marks Office and in other countries.

www.Harlequin.com

Printed in U.S.A.

Books by Sara Orwig

SARA ORWIG

lives in Oklahoma. She has a patient husband who will take her on research trips anywhere from big cities to old forts. She is an avid collector of Western history books. With a master's degree in English, Sara has written historical romance, mainstream fiction and contemporary romance. Books are beloved treasures that take Sara to magical worlds, and she loves both reading and writing them.

To my family with all my love.

One

Gabe Benton spotted the car pulled off the straight West Texas highway—a speck on the flat, mesquite-covered horizon—and he pulled to a stop expecting to find a stranger.

When he stepped out of his car, the woman, who'd been changing a flat tire, glanced over her shoulder. A thick blond braid hung beneath her baseball cap. She wore jeans and a short sleeved, cotton shirt.

"Got trouble?" he inquired.

She stood. "Gabe?" she asked in disbelief.

"Maddie?"

His heart missed a few beats. Startled to hear a voice he knew as well as his own, he looked at the woman more closely. Yes, it was Madeline Halliday, and she was even better looking now than she had been at twenty-one.

The curves shaping her white blouse were lush,

her waist tiny, her legs as long as he remembered. Her skin was creamy, stirring a vivid memory of how she had looked naked in his arms. His pulse sped up. His breathing altered. She was a knockout, now more than ever.

He was shocked at how glad he was to see her. It took an effort to resist closing the distance between them. And then he couldn't hold back. In two strides, he reached her, wrapping his arms around her, fighting the temptation to kiss her long and hard.

Their last tense week together had been six long years ago. But now Maddie was back in his life.

She was soft, warm and sweet smelling. He held her tighter, his pulse racing. When she embraced him in return and stepped back, he wanted to pull her into his arms again.

"It's great to see you," Gabe said. "You look terrific."

"Thanks, Gabe," she said.

"I'm sorry about the loss of your grandfather," he added, looking into dark brown eyes surrounded by thick lashes. After their breakup, Maddie had moved to Florida.

"Thank you. And thank you for the flowers you sent."

"The flowers were in lieu of my offering condolences in person. I'm sorry I missed the memorial, but I was in Wyoming buying cattle. By the time I got word, I couldn't have made it home in time."

"Some things don't change. You're still traveling for business," she said, and for a moment her smile faded.

"Not as much these days. Sorry I wasn't here. Sorry, too, about the loss of your father. I didn't know about his death three years ago until a year later."

"Thanks. Dad's loss was difficult. My mom has

adjusted pretty well. When I came for Granddad's memorial, there was a big crowd. Since my family has lived here almost as long as yours, there were lots of people from the area."

"What brings you back again after only three months?"

"Mom and I inherited the ranch. Neither of us wants it, so I'm here to make the arrangements to place it on the market."

"That's a surprise. I hope you've given it some thought," he said, easily falling into the closeness he had once felt with her, "because that's a fine ranch."

"We're sure about what we want to do. I hope to be back in Florida by next week and have this place sold by July."

When he grasped her hand and looked at her bare fingers, relief flooded him. "No wedding ring."

She smiled again. "No. I've been too busy with work. Let me guess—you're not wearing one either."

He grinned. "You know me too well. Will you be here long?"

"Just long enough to get everything arranged to sell. I'll stay at the ranch while I'm getting the house ready and while I find an agency to deal with the property."

"I'll finish changing your tire and then let's go where we can talk. I'll take you to dinner tonight."

She glanced at her watch. "I shouldn't—"

"Come on. You can give one evening to an old friend," he said, gazing into eyes that could, apparently, still make him weak in the knees.

"I never could resist you," she replied, smiling. "Yes," she added, and turned away, walking back to the car before he could reply.

You resisted me once was what he wanted to say, but

he kept quiet. His pulse jumped another notch now that he was reassured she was not carrying a grudge about the way they'd ended things six years ago. Already, he was anticipating the evening with her and thinking about dinner. He hurried to get to the tire before she did.

"We've lost touch," he said as he hunkered down to remove the flat. "I heard you got that business degree."

"Yes. I transferred to the University of Florida in Gainesville where I majored in business. Now I work for Clirksonie Realty in Miami."

"Like it?" he asked while he dropped a lug bolt onto the hubcap lying on the ground.

"Very much. I'm busy. I heard you moved back to the family ranch."

"I did. That year after you left, I spent more and more time there. Finally, I retired to the ranch last year. I was restless in my job and wanted the move. Maybe life wasn't the same without you here," he said, giving her a crooked grin.

She smiled, shaking her head in disbelief.

"I can't imagine you leaving your Dallas job for the ranch, but that is what you always said you wanted. I'm glad to be away from our spread. Ranching is hard work."

"Not when you love doing it. If I recall accurately, you always wanted to get away from here. Hard for me to understand. You're in Miami? No way is it as peaceful as it is out here."

She smiled. "We could argue that one forever. The ocean can be peaceful. I love the beach. I love the activity of a big city, too. Miami, Houston, Dallas— they're all exhilarating to me. I'm surprised you don't miss the office."

He shrugged. "Sometimes I do," he said. "You have grandparents in Miami, don't you?"

"Yes. My mom's parents. They're both still there and Mom is. We all live close to each other, so that's nice."

In the silence, as he worked on the flat, he couldn't help reflecting on their breakup. Maddie had been getting serious while he hadn't wanted to. When she broke off their relationship, she wouldn't talk to him or tell him why. At the time, the only disagreement between them had been his decision to accept a temporary position in Nigeria, where his company wanted to send him, rather than agree to stay in Texas with her.

It was while he was in Nigeria that he heard she'd moved to Florida. As far as he knew, the only time she'd returned to Texas was for her grandfather's memorial service.

He stood and brushed off his hands. "There," he said, carrying the flat tire to her trunk. "You picked up a nail somewhere."

"I can't imagine. This is a brand-new rental from Dallas. I got it at the airport and definitely didn't expect a flat. I've called them. They're sending out a replacement tomorrow and they'll drive this car back."

"Good deal."

"Thanks for stopping to help," she said, gazing up at him. She had pushed the baseball cap back and he looked down into her dark eyes. Strands of blond hair fluttered around her face.

"Wouldn't have missed you for the world. I'm glad to see you again. I'll pick you up at your grandfather's ranch about six."

"That's fine," she said. "Thanks again, Gabe."

He nodded and fell into step beside her as she walked

to the front of the car. He reached ahead to open the door for her, his gaze running over her as she climbed into the driver's side. After closing the door, he leaned down, speaking to her through the open window. "I'm glad you're back."

"It's only for a short time," she replied solemnly.

"I'll get you to stay longer," he said, deciding that's what he wanted.

"Still so totally confident," she said with a smile. "Another thing that hasn't changed."

"I'll see to it that you're *glad* to stay longer," he stated, smiling, but beneath his light tone, he wanted her to know that he intended to do what he said. "See you in a little while." When he stepped back, she turned the key in the ignition.

Driving home, all he could think about was Maddie. Recollections of summer evenings spent with her came back with clarity. After she'd left, it had taken him a while to admit to himself how much he missed her. He had always expected her to return home, but she never had. Until now.

Six o'clock. Would she have let him know she was back in Texas if he hadn't happened to pass her on the road? He suspected she would not have contacted him. Even so, eagerness filled him and he looked forward to the evening with her.

His ranch house loomed into sight. He'd had the place built a mile from his brother's house, which had been the family home. His brother Jake liked to stay on the ranch some of the time and they both owned shares in the ranch operation.

Gabe looked at his sprawling house. The main hall and one wing were finished. They were still working on the other wing. The roof of the house sloped over a screened-in porch, giving the structure an old-fashioned look, which he thought suited him. Every time he saw the house, it gave him satisfaction. Enough that he could almost forget that he sometimes missed Dallas.

He parked in the back and hurried to the kitchen to see what food he had stocked. He wasn't taking Maddie out to eat. Anywhere in the county she would be besieged by old friends and he wouldn't get time alone with her. She used to be warm, loving, ready for fun. He wondered how much she had changed.

God knew he'd changed in the past six years. At one time, he'd avoided all serious relationships, even with Maddie. But this past year, more and more, he'd been thinking about marriage. He'd begun avoiding long, empty nights by himself on the ranch.

His brother and his brother's friends were all married now and appeared happier than ever. His closest friend, Luke Tarkington, had married last year and Gabe saw less of him. Gabe had recently had another birthday. He was in his thirties and he'd felt a growing restlessness, an urge to settle down, but there was no one in his life he wanted to settle with.

Now, here was Maddie. He couldn't help imagining the possibilities.

When Maddie parted from Gabe, she had glanced in her rearview mirror as he walked back to his car. The same purposeful stride, the same lanky, long legs covering the ground easily. His black Stetson rested squarely on his head, the brim rolled in the typical fashion for their area of Texas. His shoulders looked broader than she remembered and she knew his lean look was deceptive, because he was stronger than a lot of men who were heavier. A persistent knot in her chest ached and she held tightly to the steering wheel as if it were a lifeline.

As she drove away, she focused on the stretch of flat highway ahead, seeing heat waves shimmer beneath the afternoon sun, too aware that Gabe was not far behind her. She waved when she turned into the Halliday ranch.

Tonight she was having dinner with Gabe.

She had always let him take charge and get his way, but she was a grown woman now and she should have refused the date.

When she had turned from her flat tire to find him standing behind her, her pulse had jumped. He was still the most handsome man she'd ever known with his startling blue eyes fringed with brown lashes. She had intended to avoid him while she was here. She definitely had not planned to spend any time with him. There was too much unresolved between them.

They had been friends since she was a kid. Later, it became so much more. Sometimes she wished she'd guarded her heart, but then she wouldn't have Rebecca. And she wouldn't have known what it was to love Gabe.

Their last summer still pained her when she thought about him walking away without making arrangements to see her again. While they had been arguing about the future, she had received the shock of her life.

The final week Gabe had been in Texas, before he'd traveled to Nigeria, she had learned she was pregnant with his baby.

Memories rushed at her now: the first shock of learning she was pregnant; the thrill of knowing she was carrying Gabe's baby. She had shared her life with Gabe since she'd been about eight, and she'd loved him almost as long. So, in some ways, the pregnancy was joyous news. It had been a bond with Gabe that was forged for life.

When she'd realized what she had to do—keep the baby a secret from him—she had been devastated. But always, no matter how she looked at the situation, the best thing for both of them had been to keep the news to herself. Gabe hadn't been ready for fatherhood or marriage or a binding commitment. He wouldn't even commit to a serious relationship with her before the pregnancy! Even now, she was still convinced that revealing the truth would have been disastrous to Gabe. She had saved them both. She'd saved Gabe from a marriage and responsibility he hadn't wanted. She'd saved herself from settling for life on the ranch when she wanted something more.

As she drove the familiar road to the home where she had grown up, she tried to ignore the tingly feeling that had started the moment she'd seen him and continued even now.

At the first sight of him her palms had gone damp and her breathing had altered. After all this time how could he still do this to her?

Memories of being in his arms, of making love to him, tormented her. Memories she had tried to forget through the years. But now that she'd seen him, they came tumbling back as fresh as if they had happened yesterday.

"I won't get involved with you again." She whispered the promise to herself, knowing that in some ways she would always be involved with him. There was Rebecca. And it had taken only one look into his blue eyes for the years to fall away. Could she still love him?

When she neared her family home, she looked at the tall wooden house that had belonged to her family for generations. She didn't mind selling it. While she had been happy here, she didn't want to move back. In Miami, she had a great place, with a big patio and a great bay-front view in a thriving metropolis she loved.

Stepping out of the car, she heard someone call her name.

She waited, watching a lanky, brown-haired man jog across the driveway toward her. Smiling, she waved.

"Maddie, welcome home."

"Thanks, Sol. You look the same as ever," she said, stepping forward to give the foreman a hug.

"Older now. It's good to have you here." He smiled at her and pushed his broad-brimmed Western hat back on his head. "How's your mom?"

"She's fine, so are my grandparents."

"You should have brought your mom with you. Tell her hello from all of us."

"I will. This is a fast business trip and then I need to get back to my work in Florida. It was easier to come by myself."

"Let me get your things. You leave all this to me." He moved past her to take her bags from the car after she opened the trunk. She shouldered a bag and picked up a suitcase.

"Leave those, Maddie. I'll get everything."

"Thanks, Sol. I'll bring this much. You can get the rest. I'm going in anyway so there's no need to go empty-handed."

"Things are in pretty good shape here. When will you have somebody out to look at the place?" he asked as they walked to the house.

"I have an appointment this afternoon in Lubbock with an agency. Tomorrow I'm meeting a broker who is driving here from Fort Worth. I have a third appointment with a representative from another agency in Dallas. I'll choose one to handle the sale and then I'll better know the schedule for placing the ranch on the market. I'm glad you've found a job you want." She entered a side door, smelling a vacant, stuffy odor as she turned off the alarm.

"Hard to leave this place, but life changes," he said, glancing around. "It's not the same with your granddad gone."

"I know it's not. It was good of you to stay for as long as I need you. It'll be a lot easier if we can sell the place as is, with cattle included and some of the furniture still in the house. If we can't sell it that way, then we'll do what we have to do. I don't know how long it'll take, but I hope we sell quickly."

"I'll pass the word along. We're down to a skeleton crew now. Most hands have taken jobs elsewhere. Some have been hired on places with the stipulation that they can't start until you've sold the ranch."

"I appreciate that," she said. "Leave the bags here at the foot of the stairs. I can get them."

"I'll take them to your room," he said, moving past her to carry the bags upstairs.

"Would you like a cup of coffee? I can have a pot brewed in no time," she called after him.

"Thanks. I'll come have coffee later if that's all right. I have to get back to work now."

She returned to the kitchen to get a glass of water and followed him to the back door. "Thanks so much for unloading my car. I'm not certain how long the arrangements will take, but I hope to get everything done this week and head back to Florida."

"The men want to say hello to you, but most of them

are out in the field right now. It's good to have you home. Sorry it isn't the happiest occasion."

"Thanks again, Sol," she said to the man who had been their ranch foreman since she was two years old.

He left, striding across the porch, jamming his hat farther down on his head.

She hurried up to the room that was still hers—white furniture, frilly white curtains, a view of the front and the big oaks that had been planted years ago by her grandfather.

She paused to stare at her canopied bed. Swamped with memories, she could envision making love in that bed with Gabe the summer she had been twenty-one. They'd had the house to themselves and she had wanted to show Gabe her home. In her bedroom, he had prowled around the room looking at everything until he drew her into his embrace for a kiss. They had made love right here, in her bedroom.

She thought now about the result of that afternoon, Rebecca. At this point in time, she couldn't guess how Gabe would feel if he discovered the truth. She suspected he'd feel the same as he would have six years ago.

Except for himself, Gabe had never really had any responsibilities. He was immensely wealthy, a millionaire; his older brother had grown up running interference between Gabe and their strong-willed father. She'd worried over her decision countless times, but she always came to the same conclusion—for her sake and for Gabe's, to save them both and to save their child from upheaval and unhappiness, Rebecca would remain a secret.

An ache deep inside started and she gave herself a small shake, closing her eyes as if that would shut out all memories of him. She busied herself unpacking and getting ready for her appointment with the agency in Lubbock.

Picking up her phone, she called home. First, she talked to her mother and then she listened to her daughter's high-pitched voice as she came on the phone.

"I miss you, Mommy," Rebecca said.

"I miss you, too," Maddie replied, feeling her insides clutch. She always hated to be away from Rebecca, especially overnight, and she missed her daughter intensely. It had been a couple of hours since the call she made after landing at DFW. She could imagine Rebecca's big blue eyes, her brown hair falling almost to her shoulders. It was Rebecca's blue eyes that would give away the truth if Gabe ever saw her. "I miss you terribly," she said.

"Come home."

"I will as soon as I can. Grandma is with you and she said you are baking cookies. You will get a cookie soon."

Maddie sat in a rocker and talked to her five-year-old for the next twenty minutes. Finally, Rebecca said goodbye and Maddie's mother, Tracie, came back on the phone. They talked another fifteen minutes before Maddie ended the call.

Touching her phone, Maddie looked at Rebecca's picture, clutching it to her heart for a moment and then staring intently at it. Long ago she had locked away wishful thinking. She had stopped imagining what might be between her and Rebecca's father, always reminding herself that Gabe was not ready for fatherhood or marriage. He probably never would be. And she had her own dreams, for a career and a life in the city. She didn't want to spend her adult life on a ranch.

These painful thoughts and memories were what she had dreaded about this trip. She'd hoped she wouldn't encounter Gabe, and now that she had, she was still certain it was best he didn't learn about his daughter. If she could get through this week, she would leave Texas for good and her heartache over Gabe would fade, as it had before.

Maddie reassured herself that she could spend this evening surrounded by old friends, cut the time short and tell Gabe goodbye early. If so, their time together would be over and she wouldn't see him again.

Two

Gabe walked across the familiar porch, remembering all the times before when he'd taken the same walk to pick up Maddie. Now, when she swung open the door, his heart pounded just as it had six years ago. She wore a dark blue, knee-length, sleeveless dress with a scoop neckline that revealed gorgeous curves. Her blond hair was caught up high on her head and fell freely in back.

His mouth went dry and he thought again that she was far more beautiful now than she had been at twenty-one. "You look fantastic," he said in a husky tone.

"Thank you. You look rather nice yourself," she added, sounding polite. "I have my purse and I'm ready to go."

Why hadn't he visited her after she moved away? He had always remembered her bitterness when they had parted and he had worked at trying to forget her. Now memories of the good times bombarded him. He'd always liked being with her. She had been gorgeous since she turned eighteen. Now she was devastating.

He inhaled an exotic scent he could not identify.

"I want to hear about the years since I last saw you," he said as he climbed into the car.

He listened while she talked about her job, her graduation from the university in Gainesville and settling in Miami where her grandparents lived. She barely mentioned her family, but he knew from past conversations that they were important to her.

"I'm still surprised to find you here. We should have kept in touch, Maddie."

"We're far apart, in years, in geographical areas, in lifestyles, in goals."

"We have a friendship that can bridge all that, and we have this attraction between us. Now that you're grown up, the years no longer matter."

"Gabe, where are we going?" she asked, looking out the side window as he turned through the front gate. "This is your ranch."

"Yep, it is. I thought I'd cook tonight. If I take you out anywhere in this county, or any of the surrounding ones, you'll have other people welcoming you back all night and guys wanting to dance and talk. I don't care to sit and watch."

She laughed. "You can't be jealous. And I know you're never bored."

"Maybe I can be."

"Which? Bored or jealous?" she asked, drawing out the word *jealous*. When he glanced at her, she smiled.

"I would be green with jealousy," he replied, flirting with her. "You're here and I want you with me exclusively. Those other guys can wait for their chances to find you with a flat tire. I'm not sharing."

She laughed, a merry sound he hadn't heard in too long. "Don't be ridiculous. You haven't seen me at all for the past six years. You have no idea who I see or if half a dozen guys are in my life."

"They aren't. You told me so earlier today," he said, grinning at her. "And for now, I know that I'm in your life and that's that."

"Still arrogant, Gabe."

"You're a gorgeous brown-eyed blonde who makes me weak in the knees. I'm not letting you out of my sight."

"I know better than to believe that 'weak in the knees' stuff."

"All right. Maybe not weak in the knees. But my heart pounds and I can't get my breath and my palms are sweaty—"

"Stop!" she exclaimed. "That's laying it on too thick."

"Or maybe I remember what great times we had together."

"We did have those," she replied with a wistful note in her voice.

"Yet I don't hear one word about you wanting to be with me, or being glad I want you all to myself, or finding this evening exciting, or anything else I would like to hear."

"I said all that when I was eighteen, nineteen and twenty," she remarked drily.

"Not enough, you didn't," he said. His insides roiled. He had been kidding and flirting, but her reaction was having a surprisingly deep impact on him.

"It's been too long, Maddie. Why didn't you come see your grandfather?"

"There was no need. He came to Florida several

times a year. He'd stay a month at a time, sometimes. The older he got the more often he came and the longer he stayed. Mom tried to get him to move there to be with all of us, but he wouldn't leave Texas. Probably felt the same way about it that you do."

"I should have called you."

"I really figured you had moved on with your life. I moved on with mine."

"You're finally a grown woman and I don't have to worry about going out with someone too young."

"As if you ever worried about that," she remarked. "It didn't keep you from asking me out."

"You were irresistible and you still are. I'm glad you're here. You're absolutely certain you don't want to keep the ranch so you can come back sometimes?"

"Positive. You know my dream has always been to get away from it."

"When you leave this time, you won't be coming back, will you?"

"No. There's no reason to return, and I wouldn't have any place to stay."

"I intend to give you a reason to want to return," he stated. "Besides, darlin', you can always bunk with me," he drawled in a husky voice, holding her hand in his. Her skin was smooth, her hand warm and soft.

"Sure, I can." She laughed, and he gave her a glance before quickly returning his attention to the ranch road. "Someday, Gabe, you might actually marry. I don't believe a wife would welcome me with open arms."

"I would," he said.

"You're still not ready to settle. Some things never change," she said. "I'm sure you're the fun loving, carefree guy you've always been."

"You say that like you're declaring I have measles.

You might be surprised. Time changes people." He looked down at her bare hand. "You haven't settled either, Maddie."

"More than you have," she said, staring out the car window.

"It will surprise you to know that I've built my own home out here."

"Now that I'll be happy to see. So you don't live with the family in the main house?"

"No. Jake and I bought Dad's shares of the ranch. I'm building because I want my own place," he said as they passed within sight of Jake's house.

"I understand that. And with your money, you don't have to worry about maintaining it or even doing your own cooking. Your dad lost interest in the ranch?"

"Dad bought a place on a lake in the Hill Country. The original house is now Jake's."

"Oh, my gosh! Is that your house?"

"Yes, it is," Gabe said.

"It's the size of a hotel," she said as he wound up the front driveway. "And they're still building," she added, staring at his home. "This is never what I would have imagined for you."

"That's interesting. What did you expect to see?"

"Something much smaller, very rustic, very masculine. You have a beautiful, old-fashioned, warm looking mansion. An enormous mansion. You can't possibly need all that space. You must be planning on marriage."

"I'm older, Maddie. Maybe it's time to settle down," he said. She turned to him. He looked at her and then back at the road. "You're shocked by my answer. A lot of space suits me and I'll have what I want in the future. It gives me room. That's one reason I love the ranch—open space. Cities feel crowded, closed in. Out here, there's peace and quiet."

"There's that, all right. You can sit and watch the grass grow. Your mansion amazes me."

"I'll have what I want in it, a theater room, a gym, an office. I'll show it to you."

"I would never have guessed you wanted something as lavish as this. Especially out here on the ranch. Landscaping, fountains. I'm sure you have a swimming pool."

"You're right. See, you don't totally have me figured out."

"I can say the same," she replied, turning to give him a direct look. As his attention swung back to the road, he wondered how much she had changed while she had been away.

He parked in front of his house, cut the engine and turned to her. "So we still have a lot to discover about each other," he said quietly.

"Don't get ideas, Gabe. It isn't going to happen. I plan to take care of business and then I'm gone forever."

"Maybe. Sometimes life can surprise you."

"May I quote you on that one?"

Her answer startled him and his eyes narrowed. "You've changed, Maddie."

"How so?"

He continued to study her, looking into her dark eyes. "You're more sophisticated, less open."

"Time and experience, I guess," she replied. While he gazed at her, silence stretched between them. For the first time since he'd known her, Maddie had an air of mystery about her. She had always been totally open with him, pouring out all her feelings. That was over.

She was poised, self-contained and self-assured, and he was more intrigued than ever.

"Come have a look at my home," he said, and climbed out of the car, hurrying to open her door. As they walked up the front steps, she looked around.

"This is a beautiful porch. A bit old-fashioned, which surprises me again," she said.

"See. There are still facets of my personality for you to discover."

"Only if I want to learn more. Because of our past, you're assuming that I do. I'm not twenty-one anymore. I grew up."

"Did you ever, Maddie," he said, his husky tone returning. "You're a gorgeous woman. My pulse doesn't stop racing when I'm around you."

"We're old friends, Gabe. That's it," she stated in such a no-nonsense tone that he felt an invisible wall between them.

"We're a hell of a lot more than that," he said, unlocking his door and turning off the alarm. He stepped back out and picked her up.

With a yelp, she wrapped an arm around his neck. "What do you think you're doing?"

"I'm carrying you across the threshold of my house as a way to welcome you. I know you're not my bride," he said, relishing holding her and breaking through the barrier she wanted to erect between them. Big brown eyes only inches from his face gazed back at him. He could detect the exotic scent she wore. Warm and soft, she was light in his arms and he didn't want to set her down. The air between them crackled with awareness and desire. The temperature in the entrance hall climbed.

Her eyes held fire in their dark depths and her lips

parted slightly. With their gazes locked, he stood her on her feet. They faced each other with only inches separating them. For him, time didn't exist. It was as if the past six years had vanished. He wanted to kiss her and she looked as if she wanted him to.

When he framed her face with his hands, she caught his wrists in each hand. "Gabe, we shouldn't go back there," she whispered.

"It's a welcome home kiss," he said, lowering his hands to her waist. He leaned closer and his mouth covered hers.

Maddie closed her eyes. She did not have the willpower to say no. She wanted his kiss, even though she knew what a hazard it would be to her peace of mind. To her whole life. She *couldn't* get involved with him again.

Yet she wrapped her arms around his waist and kissed him in return, soaring in a dizzying spiral while heat started low inside her, filling her.

Delight and desire roiled in her. Years fell away and no longer mattered. For a moment, the only significance was Gabe's mouth on hers. The man she loved—he always had been, from her first crush. In that moment, with his lips on hers, she had to face the fact that she loved him still.

Longing consumed her while his kisses enticed her to toss away caution. Her erratic breathing matched his. It was Gabe in her arms. Her tongue thrust deep. She wanted to set him ablaze as he did her.

She moaned softly in pleasure, feeling his hand drift across her shoulders. His caresses down her back and over her bottom brought her back to her senses.

"Gabe," she whispered. "We have to stop."

He raised his head slightly, the look in his blue eyes

stabbing her. "Why? You're not committed to anyone else. Neither am I. This kiss is for old times' sake and a welcome back to Texas."

She moved out of his embrace. "Don't complicate my life. I'm selling the ranch, returning to Florida and not coming back here. Don't make me want to return Texas. I don't want ties here," she said, too aware that she already had a tie to Gabe that she could never unravel.

"Those are strong words, Maddie. As if you have a grudge."

"No. I have a satisfying life in Florida that I love. I don't want it upset."

"It was only a few welcome-back kisses. You didn't want to return when it was hell of a lot more," he said. His breathing was still ragged, his blue gaze smoldering. "Come on. I'll show you around and then we'll have a drink and I'll cook steaks."

"That's fine," she answered, trying to regain her composure. She walked past him, heading for the first open door off the entrance hall. She entered a dining room. Centered below a crystal chandelier stood a table surrounded by sixteen chairs. "This is a beautiful room," she remarked.

"Don't sound so shocked. Even after you saw the exterior, you expected something rustic, didn't you?"

"Actually, yes. You've always been so into being a cowboy."

"My family room is where I went with Western furnishings. I'll show you. We'll go through the kitchen on the way."

She walked beside him through the dining room and into a spacious white kitchen. At the far end was a cozy breakfast area with another large table, a sofa and chairs, and a huge brick fireplace.

"This is wonderful, Gabe. You've done a good job. Did you plan all this yourself?"

"I had a decorator. I explained what I'd like and she did the rest. I had final approval, of course, but most of her choices suited me fine."

"This room is grand."

"Thank you. I'm glad you like it, Maddie. My office is close to the kitchen. Let me show you."

He took her down a wide hallway into a large room. He watched as Maddie surveyed the room.

"Gabe, this is amazing. Two desks. Why do you have six computers?" Without waiting for an answer, she turned to look at the rest of the room. "You have everything. Television, fax machines, copiers. You don't need this for ranching."

"I do my own investments, and I keep up with world markets. I enjoy it, and I've had some success with it."

She turned to study him. "You've surprised me again."

"I think on this one, I might have surprised my family, too."

"Does Jake consult you about investments?" she asked as her eyes narrowed.

"As a matter of fact, he does. I did a little investing for him at first. Now I do all of his personal investments."

"That's impressive."

"Not really. It's something I like, and I've been lucky. Jake and I will be worth more than Dad soon."

She inhaled, thinking about Rebecca. Gabe could do so much for his daughter. Was she doing the wrong thing, keeping Rebecca hidden from him?

"I thought we'd eat on the patio," he said, leading her back through the kitchen and outside. She stepped out to a partially enclosed, air-conditioned patio that overlooked an Olympic-size swimming pool.

"This is beautiful, too, Gabe," she said with a smile. "You can go ahead and say it. I thought I knew what kind of house you would like, but you've surprised me. A very pleasant surprise, I might add. You had an excellent decorator."

"Thanks, I think. So how different is my place from yours?"

She laughed. "My little house would fit in your dining room and kitchen. It's small and the decor is far less expensive."

"That isn't what I meant."

"It's the same style of decor."

"That's why you're so shocked. Just because I love ranching and you've always wanted to get away from Texas, you thought we were opposites in everything. What would you like to drink? I have a well stocked bar."

"How about iced tea?"

"Coming right up," he said, walking behind a bar.

She climbed on one of the high stools in front of him, crossed her legs and looked around. "You have fancy outdoor furniture, too. Do you spend a lot of time out here?" she asked, turning back and catching him looking at her legs.

"I swim often," he replied, his gaze holding hers for a long moment. While they talked about his house in a very ordinary conversation, she could still feel the tension and sparks between them. "I enjoy the patio and pool, and I'm sure I will even more as time passes."

"Except you'll be working. You'll work on the ranch and you won't relax and enjoy this any more than you do now."

"You might be right on that one. What kind of hours do you have when you're in Florida?"

"Long," she remarked drily as he handed her the iced tea. She took a sip, watching him pour his own drink and thinking of how their daughter had Gabe's coloring. What would he be like with a child? She had never seen him interacting with children.

"Let's go sit where it's more comfortable," he said.

They crossed the patio to a thickly cushioned redwood sofa. She sat in a corner and he moved close to face her.

"Tell me about your life in Miami and how it's so different from being here."

"Monday through Friday morning, I go into the office. I show houses, my time fluctuates. It's an exciting, varied job and I love it," she said, aware they sat with knees touching. Gabe had stretched out one long arm to play with locks of her hair. Each tug on her scalp made her tingle.

It was difficult to ignore the effect he had on her. Had he noticed the slight breathlessness in her voice? While she wanted to kiss him again, she couldn't afford to fall more deeply in love with him. She kept busy in Florida, finding it easier as time passed to avoid thinking about Gabe. She remembered now that when she was around him, she had little resistance. It had never occurred to her that he would bring her to his house for dinner where it would only be the two of them. A whole evening with Gabe, while her insides fizzed with excitement. She reminded herself to keep up her guard. Any feelings he created in her now would only disturb ghosts of the past she did not want disturbed.

"There has to be more than that to your life for you to love Florida so much," he said.

"Often I spend free time at the beach. My family is all nearby and I have friends. I love it. I love the city and the activity."

"Don't you still have close friends in Dallas? I remember you used to."

"Yes, I do. We keep in touch. I've even had two excellent job offers from there, one right after I graduated and one more recently."

"Did you give them any consideration?"

"Not really. I'm happy where I am. I like Dallas, and at one point in time, I would have accepted work there, but not now."

They sat and talked until Gabe put the steaks on. She strolled to the cooker with him. In minutes, spirals of gray smoke escaped from the covered grill while Gabe put bowls of tossed green salad on the table. Next, he retrieved two potatoes from the oven and they each fixed their own with butter, chives and sour cream. By the time he had steamed asparagus, the steaks were ready. They sat near a fountain on the patio.

"I'm amazed. I've never seen you do all this yourself," she said, waving her hand over the table and the food.

"I still say you don't know me as well as you think you do. Time changes people. I want to get to know you all over again, Maddie."

"Sorry, Gabe. There isn't time for it. We have tonight. That's all."

"Maybe," he said, his blue eyes intent on her.

"I had forgotten you have a stubborn streak in you."

"I think it might match the one you have," he replied with a smile. He raised his glass. "Here's to memories and new discoveries."

"Here's to seeing an old friend and wishing you a wonderful future. You're a nice guy, Gabe Benton."

One corner of his mouth lifted in a slight smile. "You keep trying to hold me at arm's length. We've been friends too long for this 'I barely know you' attitude. I'm getting past it, Maddie." On the last word, his voice lowered and the look she received made her tingle.

"Maybe. In the meantime, dinner is getting cold."

After the first bite of steak, she smiled. "This is heavenly."

"I'd rather watch you than eat," he stated.

"That's ridiculous," she replied, hating the breathlessness that fairly shouted her true reaction to him. "Besides, I'll bet you said that to the last person you invited out here."

"Truthfully, I've never said that to anyone before."

She drew in a deep breath. "It's not going to get you anywhere saying it now," she stated, glad her voice had gained a note of aloofness.

He smiled at her, shattering any illusion she might have had about him cooling his flirting.

"This is a delicious steak," she said, hoping to keep the topic neutral.

"Not nearly as delicious as your kisses."

She closed her eyes and chewed, feeling her face flush because of his remark. "I'm not listening to you. I'm eating this steak," she said. They were skirting dangerous territory. She had gotten over the past and shut Gabe out of her life. It had taken time, and it had not been easy. Now, with his flirting and charm, he was trying to get back into her life, but she had no place for him there.

"You're not looking at me, but I know you hear me," he said, laughter in his voice. "Your kisses are delicious and have taken away my appetite for what's on this table. If I hadn't found you on the highway, would you have come to Texas and then gone home to Florida without seeing me?"

As soon as he asked, her eyes flew open. She felt ensnared in his gaze. "Yes, I would have."

To her surprise, he winced. "Was it because of the way we parted?"

"Since the last summer we were together, our lives have changed. I'm different and you're different. We're really strangers now, except for childhood memories."

He leaned across the table and caught her hand lightly, rubbing his thumb over the inside of her wrist. "There's no way we're strangers, and we have a hell of a lot more than 'childhood memories' between us. You know better than that. Holding you in my arms, making love for hours under the stars—those were not childish memories," he said in a husky voice that wrapped her in a blanket of intimacy. "I thought our last summer was fantastic."

She couldn't get her breath, and she forgot about dinner. She tried to regain her composure and keep a wall up between them. She slipped her hand out of his and leaned back a fraction.

"What I want in life has changed since I left here," she said, again glad her voice held a firmness she wasn't actually feeling. She looked down at her plate blankly and then took a bite, even though her appetite had fled.

"What I want in life is changing, too, Maddie. We're older. We want different things, have different needs now than we did then. We know each other, and we don't know each other at the same time. Discovery and reunion are both great."

"Don't, Gabe," she said, shaking her head and placing her fork on her plate.

"I think that's part of you talking to me. There's still part of you who is happy to be with me."

"True enough. But the part of me that is cautious about this reunion is the intelligent, reasoning part. The part that rules my life."

He tilted her chin up and leaned close again. "Then watch out, Maddie, because I intend to cater to the other part, the emotional part that responds to me when we kiss."

"It's sheer foolishness that there are moments I can't resist you," she replied. His words had made her heart pound and now she was caught in his crystal blue gaze. Panic gripped her because she was tumbling rapidly into something she'd hoped to avoid. "We're not going to rekindle what we had. We've both moved on and our lives have changed."

"Some things haven't changed at all," he replied, running his index finger lightly down her cheek.

"I never thought we'd be having an intimate one-on-one dinner at your house tonight. You know what I expected."

"Disappointed so far?"

"You know I'm not. I want to eat and talk and remain friends. I don't want to return to being lovers."

"You eat what you want. We have the whole evening."

"I can see the plans in your eyes," she said, and shook her head. "It won't happen, Gabe."

"What do you think you can see?"

"Seduction," she stated bluntly. Her cell phone rang, and she saw it was a call from home, sending another chill down her spine. She didn't want to take the call in front of Gabe. "Will you excuse me for a moment?"

He nodded and she got up to walk away, aware he could hear the first part of her conversation as Rebecca said hello.

"Mommy, I miss you."

"Hi. What are you doing?" she asked, going into the kitchen. Her heart lurched with love at the sound of her daughter's voice. She missed Rebecca and wished she could hold her.

"I'm talking to you."

"I know you're talking to me. Are you having fun?" Maddie asked softly, assured of the answer, because Rebecca loved to spend time with her grandmother.

Maddie heard a clatter and then her mother said hello.

"Sorry, Maddie, Rebecca got the phone and called while I was running her bath. She knows which number is your one-digit call."

"That's all right. I'm eating dinner. Is everything okay?"

"We're fine. I'm getting her ready for bed. She wanted to talk to you. Now she's getting out her bath toys."

"It's always great to talk." Maddie checked over her shoulder, hoping Gabe could not hear her now.

"Are you through for today?"

"Yes. I'm out for dinner with Gabe," she said, avoiding any mention of eating at his ranch.

"Is that wise?"

She wanted to answer no, it wasn't smart at all, but she would never admit that she hadn't been able to resist his invitation. Instead, she reported the events of the day to her mother. She glanced back outside at Gabe, who sat relaxed, sipping his drink, his profile clear to her. She turned her back on him.

"I'll let you tell Rebecca good-night."

"Night, Mommy. I love you," Rebecca said.

Maddie smiled. "Night, sweet baby. I love you, too, and I miss you so-o-o much. Oodles of hugs to you," she added in a low tone.

"Come home."

"I will soon, I promise," she said, feeling an ache. Rarely away from Rebecca overnight, she missed her daughter. She switched off her phone and returned to the table, seeing the curious expression on Gabe's face.

"Call from a close friend?"

"My mother, actually," she said, sitting to finish her dinner. "She expected to find me alone."

"Do you live close to your mother?" he asked, and she noticed he was not eating.

"Very close. She's next door."

"That makes it easy," he said.

"I heard your brother married Caitlin Santerre."

"That's right. Jake is very happily married as of this past winter. Caitlin is a freelance photographer with her own galleries. She's very good. And, yes, she is a Santerre."

"That was a shock. I thought maybe someone got it wrong. A Benton marrying a Santerre. End of the feud."

"Unless Will Santerre returns to Texas, but he told Jake he never would. He sold the family ranch to Jake and now we've got an oil well."

"Which I'm sure fell into your line of work."

"Yes, it did. Jake was getting to be a menace to himself at work, he was so crazy in love."

"Which you've always managed to avoid."

"Maybe I was waiting for you to come home," he said, leaning closer to run his finger along her cheek again.

She wrinkled her nose at him. "I know better than

that, too. There's really only one person in your life, and that is Gabriel Benton."

"I'm a bachelor. It goes with the territory."

"So when you decided to retire from the corporate world and live on the ranch, name the people you consulted about your decision?"

He shook his head. "You got me on that one. I didn't consult anyone."

"That's right. Gabriel Benton is the only one involved. Enough said."

"I don't recall you being tough or cynical. I remember someone sweet as sugar."

"I've been out in the real world a while."

"If you're through eating, let's move elsewhere."

"It was a wonderful dinner. What a good husband you'll make someday," she said with amusement.

"I'm glad to hear you admit that," he answered. "Bring your drink and let me show you something else."

Perplexed, wondering where they were going, she picked up her iced tea and followed him down the hall. They entered a large billiard room with polished oak floors. A billiard table stood to one side of the room. Gabe switched on a few low lights and turned on music.

He crossed the room to take her drink and set it on a table. "Let's dance."

A two-step played. She hadn't danced one in years, so she faced him and they danced on the open floor beside the billiard table.

He spun her around and pulled her close, his boots scraping on the oak floor.

When the dance ended she laughed. "That was great, Gabe. I haven't danced a two-step in too long to remember."

"A polka's up next."

Maddie's cell phone rang and she pulled it out of a pocket and waved it at him. "If you'll excuse me," she said, turning and walking into the hall to talk.

When she returned, a ballad was playing. Gabe stepped close. He put one hand on her waist and he held her hand with his other one.

"Sorry about the call," she said. "Work."

"That's fine. Take all the calls you want. I don't mind."

"Thanks." As they danced, she looked up and was mesmerized. She was dancing in Gabe's arms again. It brought back too many memories.

"Things were good between us, Maddie," he said solemnly.

"I know they were, until we parted. Then they weren't. Soon I had left here and you did, too."

"I remember when you were a little kid. When your dad brought you to our ranch, you'd follow me everywhere I went."

"Thank heavens I outgrew that!"

He smiled at her. "I'd be happy for you to follow me everywhere now."

"I don't think you mean that for one second. It won't happen anyway, so we'll never really know."

He turned a long lock of Maddie's blond hair in his fingers. "Your hair was probably the envy of all the girls in school."

"I don't think so."

"It's gorgeous now."

"Thank you."

"Remember when we'd meet and have those early morning rides at sunrise—something I haven't done in years."

"Neither have I, but that I don't miss. Life changes, Gabe."

He pulled her closer and they danced in silence. They had always danced well together. She remembered how easy it had been to follow his lead. Being in his arms, dancing with him, spending time with him—every moment reawakened memories and brought back ties she thought she had severed. *Get through the night and tell him goodbye.*

When the ballad ended and another began, Gabe looked down at her. Their gazes met and the air between them crackled with electricity. His arm around her waist tightened, and he started to kiss her.

"This is where I need to say no, no, no, although I can't imagine it would have any effect if I did," she whispered.

"You don't really want to say no," he said, and then kissed her. His arms banded her waist while she wrapped hers around his neck. His tongue went deeply into her mouth, stroking, stirring memories, creating new ones.

Time spun away while they kissed. She wanted him more with each breath, but she knew she couldn't get involved with him. Her future—Rebecca's future—depended on avoiding that.

He ran his hand down her back, caressing her bottom lightly. His hand drifted up again while he continued to kiss her senseless.

How long they kissed, she didn't know. Still kissing her, Gabe picked her up and carried her to the sofa. He sat, cradling her on his lap.

Her heart pounded and she ached inside, deep down. Physically, she wanted him with all her being. But logically, it was the cold, hard truth that getting entangled with Gabe would ruin the life she'd built. She had a secret child to keep from him. Intimacy would only lead him to discover the truth.

Gabe caressed her nape and passion once more consumed her. She wound her fingers in his thick hair and unfastened the buttons of his white shirt with her other hand. In minutes, she'd pushed away the white shirt and toyed with his brown chest hair while they continued kissing.

Gabe's hand moved to her throat and then slipped lower, following the curve of the neckline of her dress.

She gasped with pleasure and then moaned softly. For a moment, she relished his caresses. She was with the man she had loved all her life. How easy it would be to pick up where they'd left off. And how disastrous. She gripped his wrist, moving his hand.

"This has to stop," she declared, gasping for breath. "That summer you left—I won't go through that again." She sat up, straightening her dress. His blue eyes were filled with fire. Locks of his brown hair tumbled on his forehead.

"It was only a few kisses," he said quietly. "It's not the same as that summer. And back then, I needed to leave, for my job."

"That's over and done, but I don't ever want to feel that way again." She stood and smoothed her dress.

"I was only in Nigeria for eight months. You could have continued your education at Tech, and when I returned, I'd have been there for you."

"Gabe, it's ridiculous to argue now, but you would not have 'been there for me,'" she said. "You were never into commitment, and you certainly weren't at that point in your life. And I was."

"I suppose you're right on all counts," he admitted,

surprising her. He stood. "I'll get our drinks. Come sit here and we can talk."

She returned to the sofa. Gabe picked up his cold bottle of beer and joined her, sitting close. He took a sip and turned to face her.

They sat and talked until almost midnight. She asked about the last rodeo he had participated in, listening and laughing as he talked about his bronc riding. That led to what she had been doing and she told him about her family trip to France and Italy and how much she had enjoyed the cathedrals she had seen. Finally, when she saw it was only minutes until midnight, she said, "I should get home now. I don't usually stay out late. If my family should call me, they would be in a panic if I'm not home."

"Your mother surely won't call at this hour. Besides, she obviously knows to try your cell phone. I remember she kept close track of you, but you're a grown woman now."

"She still worries. She wasn't happy about my plans to stay alone at the ranch. I think she's forgotten how safe it is here."

"You know you can stay right here with me."

"Oh, right. As if that would be a peaceful night's rest."

She gave him an exasperated glare.

He threw up his hands. "Okay. I know that look. I'll take you back to your ranch now."

She smiled. "I knew you'd do what I asked. Thank you, Gabe," she said sweetly.

He picked her up and spun her around. She yelped while she clung to his shoulders. "Hey!"

"I'm glad to see you and wanted to do that one more time. I wanted to hold you and have you hold me. I wanted to hear you laugh. Maddie, I'm glad you're back," he said, suddenly sounding earnest. Her heart lurched.

"I'm not really back. I left your life a long time ago," she replied, feeling the tension escalate between them once again.

He inhaled deeply. "I'm going to change your mind about leaving again." The note of steel in his tone made her heart beat faster. Once, she would have been thrilled to hear those words from him. Now, they threatened her peaceful life.

"Don't try to make a project of me. Besides, you haven't missed me."

"I did miss you," he said. "I just didn't realize how much. You've been in my life even when we were both kids. When you moved away, you left a void."

His words wrapped around her, binding her heart to him in ways she wouldn't be able to forget. In ways she couldn't deal with now. "Gabe, you don't mean it. You would have come after me if you'd felt that strongly."

"It took a long time for me to realize the cause of my dissatisfaction. Even longer to face that my life had changed because you were no longer in it."

"I need to get home," she said abruptly. She didn't want another broken heart. It had taken her years to mend her last one.

He leaned forward to touch her lips with his again, a fiery, possessive kiss that bound her heart as tightly as his words had.

When he raised his head, she looked into determined blue eyes. He set her on her feet and their gazes still held. With an effort, she turned toward the door.

They walked through the house together and out to his car. When they stepped into the cool night, Gabe draped his arm across her shoulders and pulled her close against him.

"Anyone who works for you staying at the house with you?"

"No, there's no one staying with me."

"In all seriousness, you could stay here, you know. You can have a separate bedroom, and you'll have all the peace and quiet and privacy you want."

"I better stay at my place," she replied, doing the smart thing. "I've always felt safe at home. Besides, I have a direct line to Sol's house."

"That's good to know. He'd come on the run if you needed him."

At the car, Gabe turned her to face him, keeping his arm around her.

"Let me take you to dinner again tomorrow night. I won't bring you over here. We'll go somewhere special."

"Thanks, Gabe. Tonight was great. You know I had a great time—"

"Maddie, let's have another few hours together," he said, interrupting what she had been about to say. "A dinner is harmless. You'll sell the place soon. You could sell it by the weekend, and then you'll return to Florida. Let's go out together again before you leave," he said, bending his knees so he could look into her eyes.

She argued with herself, a tiny voice screaming to turn him down. That voice was being drowned out by another inner voice shouting yes. And Gabe was looking at her with those sexy blue eyes that spun a magic spell.

"Yes, Gabe. Against all logic and good judgment, I'll have dinner with you again."

He gave her a tiny squeeze. "I'm glad. We'll have a super time." He leaned forward to brush a kiss on her forehead, then her lips.

He held open the passenger-side door for her, closed it and strode around the car to slide behind the wheel. They talked all the way to her ranch and then sat in the driveway talking for another hour. It was into the early-morning hours when he walked her to the door.

He entered with her and waited while she switched off her alarm and turned on the lights. "It's been a great evening, Maddie. I'm glad you're back, even if it's temporary." Stepping closer, he brushed another kiss on her lips. His mouth was warm, enticing, coaxing more kisses.

"Gabe," she said, ending the kiss.

He looked over her head to the room beyond her. "This is a big house out in a remote spot. You're accustomed to a big city, a house with neighbors, your mother close by. I'll sleep down here on the couch."

"Sol is not far away."

"He's about four minutes if he comes on a dead run. I can stretch out on the sofa and you'll never know I'm here."

"I'm not a little kid any longer. You don't have to protect me and hover around."

"I'll be the one to decide about hovering and I know you are definitely not a little kid any longer. I've known that since you were seventeen," he drawled in a softer tone that caused her belly to flutter.

"In the morning, I have an appointment in town at nine o'clock."

"I can call you way earlier than that. Or I can tiptoe out before you wake up."

"Gabe, I'll be fine."

"I know, but I'll worry. Your mother will feel better—even Sol would say it's a good idea. Now, no more arguments. I'm on the sofa."

She shook her head. "If you get kinks in your back, it's your own fault. There's nothing yummy here for breakfast because I drink coffee and orange juice and eat a piece of toast. Without butter."

"Fine with me."

She stood with her hands on her hips, staring at him in consternation, certain she would not shake him out of the house tonight. "Gabe, you know it's as safe here as if I were sleeping in the middle of the sheriff's office."

"It will be, with me here," he replied, grinning.

She shook her head in exasperation. "I'll lock up and then I'm going upstairs to bed."

"Fine and dandy. I'll stay downstairs. I remember my way around."

"Do you really?" she asked, surprised. She threw up her hands. "Stay. I'll be up at six. I'll let you out and lock the door behind you. I'm not getting you a pillow or anything, Gabe. I don't want you doing this."

He smiled. "I won't worry. Sol won't worry, because he'll see my car and you can tell him that I slept on the sofa."

"I'm not telling Sol anything."

"Suit yourself, Maddie. 'Night." Gabe brushed a kiss on her lips and headed off to the front living room.

She shook her head, locked up and went upstairs, leaving the downstairs lights on for Gabe to worry with.

She was going out with him again. She rubbed her forehead and glanced over her shoulder, seeing the light still spilling from the front room. He'd always been so protective! He had a strong sense of duty. Six years ago, she had been certain that if she told him about her pregnancy, he would have insisted they marry out of a misguided sense of honor. He would have been far more stubborn and insistent about that than he had been about staying tonight. And her future would have been as ruined as his. Even after seeing how much he'd changed, and even though she wished Rebecca knew her father, she still felt justified in her actions.

The evening had been exciting—and dangerous to her heart. Gabe was older now and, to her surprise, he had grown more responsible, even more appealing than he had been before. He had changed. His house had been a big shock, not at all what she'd expected. And he'd missed her—she was still trying to hold that at bay.

Maybe they both had grown up during their years of separation. And if it turned out Gabe *had* grown up, she might have to rethink the future.

She thought of Rebecca again, unable to keep from wondering what it would be like if the three of them were together.

Three

Stretched out on the sofa, Gabe reflected on what he had admitted to Maddie—something he had never said aloud before in his life. Not even to his brother, Jake, the person he was the closest to. He hadn't wanted to face the truth six years ago: that Maddie's departure was the source of his dissatisfaction with life. It had taken him a long time to realize that his restlessness had only started after he'd returned home to find that Maddie had moved to Florida.

He didn't know whether or not she had believed him tonight, but he had been truthful. He had missed her. He hadn't gone after her because, at first, she'd ended the relationship before either of them left West Texas. And, then, he had thought she'd come back to Texas. Once time had passed, he hadn't been sure of his welcome. But now he knew that she still responded to

him physically. He expected to overcome the barriers
she kept putting between them.

Maddie had emphatically declared there was no
man in her life, but he wondered. Each time she had
answered her cell phone, she had spoken in a soft,
guarded voice. She had not been talking to her mother,
or a grandmother either. Not in that deep, soft tone.
Both calls had come from someone she cared about.

His thoughts shifted to the coming day. He was
meeting his brother and his brother's best friends for
breakfast in Dallas at seven. He'd have to take his small
plane. And he'd have to get out of Maddie's house before
six, but night would be over.

Six o'clock was only a few hours away, but sleep
wouldn't come. He couldn't get Maddie out of his
thoughts. If she sold the ranch and left, he would go
to Florida to see her this time. He wouldn't let her
disappear from his life again.

With that determination still fresh in his mind,
Gabe left for Dallas the next morning without waking
Maddie.

He walked into the restaurant several minutes late
and spotted his brother and friends sitting at a large
round table in the corner. Gabe had always tagged along
with Jake and his buddies. Growing up, he had been the
younger brother and they had put up with him. Once
grown, the slight difference in their ages no longer
mattered. Gabe had become close friends with Tony
Ryder, a driven, near-billionaire hotel magnate who
had recently married. With thick, unruly black curls
and dark eyes, Tony looked more like a Vegas roulette
dealer than the tough businessman he was.

Nick Rafford had been the first in the group to marry
and had wed the woman who had adopted his deceased

brother's baby. Now they had their own little girl and Nick seemed more relaxed, happier. Gabe wondered if that would happen to Jake because of his marriage.

As Gabe hurried to join them, Jake saw him coming and stood to greet him. "Good morning. Here's my cowboy brother," he said, smiling at Gabe, who had dressed in slacks, but wore his broad-brimmed hat and his Western boots. Gabe shook hands with his older brother, feeling as close to Jake as he thought it was possible to feel. Jake had always included Gabe in things he did.

Dressed in suits, the others would leave for work as soon as breakfast was over. Gabe went around the table to shake hands with each man

"Sorry, I got a little delayed."

"We're used to it. Brother even ordered for you," Nick remarked drily.

Gabe turned to Jake. "So what did you order?"

"Your usual—pancakes, poached egg, bacon, orange juice."

"Sounds good, thanks. How are all the families?" he asked, and listened as each one answered, with Nick producing pictures of his two children, Michael and Emily.

"Jake, tell him your news before one of us does," Tony said.

"What don't I know that everyone else does?" Gabe asked his brother, realizing Jake hadn't stopped smiling since saying hello.

"Caitlin is expecting a child," Jake said, grinning broadly. "You're going to be an uncle, kid brother."

"Congratulations!" Gabe said, delighted. "Imagine, me—an uncle." He grinned nearly as broadly as Jake. "That is fantastic news! Astounding."

"I didn't expect this much enthusiasm from a guy who knows nothing about babies." Jake studied his brother.

"I like Nick's kids. Michael is cute, and Emily is a little doll."

"Thanks. I have to agree," Nick replied with a grin.

"Maybe you're growing up, Gabe," Jake said, still focusing on his brother.

Gabe laughed. "This baby is different, too. This will be my nephew. Or niece," he added. "I might have a niece. Wow. If we weren't in this relatively quiet restaurant, I would let out a whoop."

"Hold it in, little brother," Jake drawled. "I know you, and you're not kidding. If you do that in this place, we'll get booted out before we get breakfast. Celebrate when you get outside."

"Let's have a toast," Gabe said, raising his glass of water. "To my brother and to Caitlin. Congratulations to the new mom and dad. May you always remember not to meddle unnecessarily in your baby's life."

"Hear, hear," Nick said, smiling as they all clinked glasses of water against Jake's goblet.

"Amen to that one," Tony added. "With all our interfering fathers, I hope we have learned to stay out of our children's lives when we should. Course, our control freak dads were what made us all such close friends through the years. Because of them, we have a bond that most men don't. But as much as I like y'all, I'd rather not have that tie with you."

"Well, thank goodness Dad still leaves me alone," Gabe said as he set down his glass.

"He sees you as the baby brother and doesn't realize time is passing. When you take the plunge and propose, he'll go into shock," Jake said with another smile.

"You're right," Gabe replied, thinking about Maddie. He glanced around the table and looked at three happy men who were more relaxed than they used to be in their single days. "I will have to admit, marriage seems to agree with the three of you."

"That and the recent investments you've made for us," Tony said, raising his glass to Gabe. "You've made us all richer. I knew there must be a good reason I put up with you tagging along all those years. Who knew then you'd grow up to be a shrewd investor?"

"Maybe his brother," Nick said. "Jake always has had faith in you. Thanks, Gabe. You've really turned a dollar for us."

"See, I kept telling y'all if you put up with him, you'd be glad someday," Jake said, and they all laughed.

"I'm glad everyone is happy," Gabe said, looking up as the waitstaff brought big trays loaded with breakfast.

"Thanks again for ordering for me, Jake."

"You're welcome. You're predictable when it comes to breakfast. About the only thing predictable in your life."

Gabe grinned. "Speaking of unpredictability, Maddie Halliday is back. She's come home to sell the Halliday ranch. Don't get a gleam in your eye, Jake. You own more land than one man should right now."

"I may not be able to resist looking at the ranch, *Dad,*" Jake said.

"I deserve that one. Buy the Halliday place if you want it. It isn't close to yours though."

"That won't matter. I'll look into it. Is it on the market?"

"Not yet. That's what Maddie's here to do. I happened along yesterday when she was on her way to the ranch and had a flat on her brand-new rental car."

"What's she up to? Is she married?"

"No, she's not."

"Well, well," Jake said, studying his younger brother.

"I can see the wheels turning, Jake. She loves Florida and her job there. Her mother and maternal grandparents all live there. She can't wait to put the ranch on the market and get out of here forever."

"No, I don't guess there will be anything between the two of you, then. Her determination to leave Texas would kill any interest you would have in her," Jake said.

Conversation changed and Gabe was happy to eat in silence and avoid more questions about Maddie. For now, he wasn't sharing his thoughts with Jake.

When the group had finished eating and broken up to go to work, Jake walked out with Gabe.

"I wasn't kidding about looking at the Halliday ranch," Jake said. "Actually, I'm surprised you don't want it. It's closer to your half of the ranch than mine."

"Jake, I'm spending more time with my investments. And yours, I might add. I'd rather do that than worry about increasing my land holdings."

"I'd rather you did, too. You're a damn fine petroleum engineer, but you've got the knack for investments— that's your real talent. Just keep it up. You're going to make me wealthier than Dad and probably yourself, too. He'll go into shock when he realizes the extent of how your wealth has increased. I've told him a little, and he gets very quiet."

"I like the work, Jake. Anyway, I don't have to own half of West Texas to be satisfied. Our ranch is big enough, and we've got income from other sources. To me, it just looks like a lot more work. The Halliday ranch may turn a tidy profit, but I can't see why you'd want to deal with it. "

Jake studied him a moment. "The door is always open at the office. You know I'd like to have you on a consulting basis if you don't want to come back full-time."

"Thanks."

"The guys were talking before you arrived today. They are really happy, Gabe. You've done a great job for them."

"I'm doing all right for myself. Investing is a way to prove myself, beyond the family business and the ranch. I'm no longer 'Jake's little brother.' It's one thing that I've done all on my own, with no family involvement other than the fact that you are one of my clients."

"You hardly have to prove yourself."

"Sometimes I feel I do. Jake, I've always been your little brother. That's how people know me. This is something I can do that is totally apart from the family business or the family ranch or your expertise. I'm on my own."

"Well, if it makes you feel better, you've been damned good at it. You're making both of us billionaires. I think it's only a matter of time until Dad asks you to handle some of his personal investments."

"I wouldn't mind that," Gabe said, and then he wanted to change the subject. "I'm thrilled for you and Caitlin. The baby is really great news."

Jake grinned. "We think so. We're excited. Actually, Mom and Dad are far more worked up than I thought they'd be."

"Mom, I'm not surprised. Now Dad—he'll be a granddad. I wonder if that gave him a jolt."

"Didn't seem to. So far he hasn't tried to interfere, but I expect an account to open soon for our baby."

"Oh, sure. He'll do all sorts of things. Tell Caitlin I'm happy for both of you. And thrilled for me. An uncle. Most amazing. Can't wait to spoil him or her. Dad may not be the only one starting to do things for the baby."

Jake laughed. "You surprise me more all the time. Could it be my baby brother is growing up?"

"Maybe it's time, Jake," Gabe answered a little more sharply than he'd intended.

"How do I get in touch with Maddie?" Jake asked.

"I have her cell phone number," Gabe replied, fishing in his pocket for his billfold and pulling out a slip of paper with her number. "Here, call her on my phone, and I'll talk to her after you've finished."

"Sure," Jake replied, making the call and setting up an appointment with her to discuss the ranch. He handed the phone to Gabe. "Thanks. She's waiting. See you, Gabe."

Gabe nodded as he said hello to Maddie, watching his brother walk away and thinking about the baby news. Jake would be a dad, and he would be an uncle.

He sauntered to his car and climbed in, sitting and talking to Maddie, reminding her they were going to have dinner at a local place where she would see a lot of her friends.

Maddie had an appointment, so as soon as they finished their call, Gabe drove to a local jewelry store to find a baby gift for Jake and Caitlin, finally settling on a Dresden calliope music box that he had gift wrapped. Whistling, he drove to the office, still amazed that he would soon be an uncle, something he had never thought about and hadn't expected to have happen for a long time.

Maddie would be as surprised as he. An hour after lunch, Gabe was already wanting to leave early so he could get ready to see her and tell her the good news.

Maddie dressed in new jeans and a blue Western shirt. She looked forward to the evening and getting out where she could see old friends. She tried to keep that prospect as her focus and avoid thinking about Gabe, but it was impossible.

"Foolish, foolish woman," she admonished herself, speaking aloud in the empty room. When she had come home for her grandfather's funeral, six men had asked her out. She had turned each one down. She hadn't wanted to go out with them, but even if she had, she still would have refused to do so. Any relationship in these parts would complicate her life too much. Besides, next to Gabe, the men all paled in comparison.

"Why can't you fall in love with someone else?" she asked herself, thinking about Gabe.

The doorbell rang and she hurried downstairs to open the front door. Looking great, Gabe stepped inside.

"Oh, my word." Her gaze raked over his blue shirt and his tight jeans and Western boots. "We're dressed alike," she observed, making him flash a wicked grin.

"We think alike," he said.

"Oh, no we don't. I know better than that. I'll run and change my shirt. You stay right here. Or go sit in that front room where you used to wait for me."

He gripped her wrist. "Forget it. You look great and I'm happy for us to be dressed alike. Maybe it'll send a message to the locals to stay away from you."

She stared at him a few seconds before she spoke. "I cannot understand you. You act like you want a relationship between us, yet I know you don't."

"Oh, yes, I do. I keep telling you—time and people change. You're different now, and I am, too. So let's explore the differences."

Sighing, she shook her head. "Gabe, don't try to dredge up what's over."

"We can talk in the limo. Are you ready to go?"

"I suppose, although I think we'll look silly dressed alike."

His grin returned. "I like it. Makes you my woman."

"If that doesn't sound like a Neanderthal, I don't know what would. You're not going to ruin my evening out, are you?"

"No, I'm going to stand back and watch every single guy in the county want to dance with you."

She had to smile. "I suspect a few ladies will see to it that you don't get lonesome while I'm on the dance floor."

They both laughed, and he squeezed her hand lightly. "It's great to be together again," he said. His words twisted her insides. She didn't want to have fun with him, fall into old habits and find him as charming as ever. Why did he always seem larger than life to her? It had made sense when she had been eight years old and he had been thirteen. Back then, she had thought of him as the big brother she wished she had. She stopped seeing him as a substitute brother when she was about twelve years old. By that time, she thought Gabe was the cutest boy in the next dozen counties.

As they sped along the highway, Maddie talked about the agencies she'd interviewed earlier that day, and Gabe told her what he knew about each and which one his family used.

"Enough about me and my day. How was yours?"

He flashed her a broad grin, and she wondered

if he had made some highly rewarding deal. "What happened? You look like the proverbial cat."

"Happier than any cat. I got some really great news. Jake is going to be a father, which means I will be an uncle."

While he shot her another quick smile, she stared in surprise. "That's really great," she said.

"You don't sound like you actually think so," he said, giving her another quick look.

"Again, you shock me. I'm amazed you're so delighted. What do you know about babies or being an uncle?" she asked with a sharp note in her voice.

"Nothing," he replied cheerfully, "but I'll learn and it'll be fun. I'm excited to be an uncle." He gave her another quick look. "Sorry, Maddie. For a moment I forgot you're an only child, so you won't be an aunt."

"I'm not worried about that. I could marry someone who is an uncle, and then I would be an aunt by marriage. I'm amazed that you find a baby really great news. I figured you wouldn't care."

"Maybe a few years ago I would have been that way, but this spring I volunteered to help with a shelter after a tornado, and those little kids were cute. Then I got involved in a community project where we took two kids to work on the ranch, and I dealt with them pretty much on a daily basis. I enjoyed both projects."

"Well, another surprise. I didn't know you were into good deeds, and I'm astounded you enjoyed working with the kids."

"See, I've been telling you since yesterday, there are facets to me that you don't know."

"Maybe there are, Gabe," she said, looking at him intently, wondering if he had changed. She had known him extremely well by the time she moved away from Texas. At that time, he had no interest in kids, commitment or charitable deeds.

"Now, I can't imagine my brother as a father, but Jake will be a good one, I'm sure," Gabe said.

"I'm sure, too. He's been like a father to you," she said.

It was hard to imagine the Gabe she used to know donating his time to help storm victims and enjoying spending time with kids. Also, the project that had involved kids at his ranch would have meant an even stronger mentorship with the kids. Had he matured and grown up in the years she hadn't seen him? Would his feelings toward his own status as a dad be different now than they would have been six years ago?

For the first time, she began to seriously question the stand she had taken to keep Rebecca's existence a secret from her father. If Gabe had changed, her decision to keep Rebecca a secret would have to transform, too. She glanced at his profile and wondered again about the depth of his feelings about the expected baby arriving in his family.

Her world had suddenly shifted. She was at a loss and needed to regain her composure before Gabe noticed. He used to be able to read all of her feelings.

"Have you talked to Caitlin yet?"

"No, but I will soon. I got a baby present this morning, and I had it gift wrapped. If I'd thought a minute, I would have held off on the wrapping and shown it to you."

"One more surprise. What did you buy?"

"It's a fancy calliope music box from Starling's Jewelry."

"I'll bet it's beautiful. The baby can't touch it, but

that's sweet, Gabe. Caitlin and Jake can play it for the little one. That was being a good uncle."

"I can't wait. A nephew would be fun. A niece—that would be a huge delight."

Thinking instantly of Rebecca, Maddie's heart thudded. She drew a deep breath. Again, she questioned her decision to keep Rebecca from her father. If Gabe was this way about Jake's baby, what would he be like about his own? Had she made a terrible mistake? Or had Gabe matured over the past six years?

He kept talking to her, but she couldn't focus on what he was saying. Her ears rang, and she felt lightheaded. She tried to get a grip on her emotions. Gabe had shocked her deeply, and he was going to realize something was amiss if she didn't begin to act like herself.

After a few more seconds, she picked up the thread of conversation.

Gabe drove her to a local place where musicians were already playing fiddles and people were doing the two-step. They hadn't gone three feet from the front door before old friends greeted and hugged Maddie.

Gabe left her with friends and managed to get a table. He ordered an iced tea for her and a cold beer for him then returned to stand near her.

Finally, they made it to their table. Gabe glanced at his watch. "That only took a half hour. Think I'll get to dance with you tonight?"

Smiling, she grasped his hand. "Let's go dance now."

They entered the dance floor while a two-step was playing. Gabe was a great partner, and she loved dancing with him. With work and Rebecca, she had missed going dancing. When Gabe faced her, his blue-eyed gaze blazed with desire. She couldn't look away.

Her racing heartbeat and breathlessness were not from dancing.

They finished the dance and another couple hurried over to greet her. She hugged Sophie, her closest friend from early childhood, and then received a light hug from Sophie's husband, Tyler Randolph, another local she had known most of her life. Her past was secret from old Texas friends, which always gave her a twinge of guilt. Her grandfather had been a man with secrets and he kept them well, including the one concerning his granddaughter.

They chatted until music started again.

The next dance was claimed by another local she had grown up with. While she danced with Dan Emerson and caught up on his life, she saw Gabe dance by with another acquaintance. Molly was laughing at something Gabe was telling her, and he was smiling. He looked as if he were having the time of his life. This was Gabe as she had always known him—fun, carefree, charming, enjoying life to the hilt. And not a man for marriage, babies, responsibility—as carefree as the wind. Was she missing what was really there? Had life and time made changes in him?

Later in the evening, they ordered ribs, but she could barely get through her dinner for people coming over to talk to her. They soon had half a dozen chairs around their table.

It was midnight when she finally agreed to leave. Not until they were in his pickup, did Gabe give her a long look. "I've finally got you to myself."

"Sorry, Gabe. Is it really that important to you to have me to yourself? I had a wonderful time seeing old friends."

"I'm glad you did, even though I wanted your undivided attention."

"It was nice to see everyone. Except for a few close friends in Dallas, I only kept in touch with Granddad. My family ties here are severed. By the way, I meant to tell you, your brother and I have an appointment. He said you knew that he was interested in our ranch."

"That's right. Jake is buying up Texas."

She smiled. "Funny he's doing that when he doesn't even live out here all the time and doesn't sound enthused about ranch life the way you do."

"No, he doesn't love it to the extent I do, but Jake loves being on the ranch as a getaway. He can relax out here. This land grab is Jake's means of going after oil, gas and water—natural resources that he expects to become more valuable each year."

"Your brother has the Midas touch. I hope that you inherited it, too."

"Enough to keep me happy. Jake does the work of two men. Since his marriage, he's a little better about taking time off. Would you object to selling to him?"

"Not at all if the price is right. I'd be happy to sell to your brother, and it would probably have pleased my grandfather. I want to be rid of the ranch and go home."

"I'll never understand your attitude about Texas. You were happy growing up here."

"I love the bustle and excitement of a big city so much more. I always have. I love Dallas, Houston, Miami. Had I stayed in Texas, I would have settled in Dallas most likely."

"I wish you had. I have a feeling you'll make the sale soon and be gone. I'll come see you in Florida this time," he promised.

"If you come, I think you'll be disappointed because I give myself completely to my work."

Her cell phone rang, and she looked at it. "I need to answer this call." She spoke softly, but knew Gabe could hear her easily. "Good night. That's great. I miss you, too," she said in almost a whisper. "Is everything okay?" She listened to Rebecca talking and then said her farewell. "I love you, too. 'Night."

"Your mother really misses you, doesn't she?" Gabe asked, sounding nonchalant, but she could tell he didn't think she had been talking to her mother.

"Yes, she does," Maddie answered. "We have always been close."

"Nice, that you two are close. I wouldn't want to be so close with my parents. I love them, but they meddle. Especially with Jake's life."

"Is your dad still doing that?" she asked, hoping to divert the conversation away from her phone call. "I remember some of the times you told me about the grief he gave your brother."

"My dad laid down an ultimatum for my brother last year. Jake had to marry within the year or he would be disinherited."

"Good heavens. That's dreadful," she said. "I remember you complaining sometimes about your dad interfering with you, but nothing that drastic. Is he interfering with you now?"

"No. Not so far. He's always concentrated on Jake."

"Why did he want Jake to marry so badly? Did he want a grandbaby?" she asked, tilting her head to one side to study Gabe.

"I'm sure. Now that Jake and Caitlin have announced they're expecting, my parents will have their first grandchild and be focused on that. I expect my dad to stop meddling with Jake and hopefully never start with me."

Gabe parked in the driveway near the back entrance to her house. Porch lights were on and a tall yard lamp spilled yellow light in a large circle over where they had parked.

As soon as she unlocked the door and they stepped inside, Gabe drew her into his embrace and kissed her. She clung to him tightly, too many memories pressing in, desire running wildly rampant.

"Maddie," he whispered.

Her insides heated. She wanted him with a desperation charged with six years of empty nights and tormenting dreams. After being reminded of all she'd left behind tonight, now, Gabe was in her arms, kissing her and she didn't want to let him go. For a few minutes, she stopped thinking with logic and reason. Instead, she took what she wanted and gave herself to him.

He raised his head, combing his fingers into her hair, pushing out her pins and letting it fall freely. "Ah, Maddie, this is what's right, the way it should be," he whispered, showering kisses on her as her hair cascaded over her shoulders.

She had to stop, but not yet. For now, she relished being in Gabe's arms, kissing him, touching him and being touched by him.

"I can't go back into an intimate relationship," she whispered. "We—"

His mouth ended her talk.

She caressed his nape, his throat while she swiftly unbuttoned his shirt and pushed it off his shoulders to run her hands over his muscled, broad shoulders. He had filled out since he was twenty-seven. He was more muscular, firm, sleek and enticing.

She wrapped her arms around his neck again to kiss him, because this was Gabe, the love of her life. On fire with wanting him, she closed her eyes and stopped thinking, giving herself to heightened awareness of his mouth on hers, his hands moving over her, his strong, powerful body.

"This is right. You belong with me," he whispered, startling her. He had never before made such a remark.

"This can't happen," she whispered. "I wanted to avoid this."

"You won't have regrets," he said.

"You were always too arrogant. There is no way I 'belong' to you, Gabe," she said, meaning it, yet unable to stop kissing him.

Gabe kissed her again, and logic spun away. While she held him tightly, relishing the moment, she drew one hand down his smooth, muscled back. She felt his fingers at the buttons of her shirt and in seconds he'd tugged it off and tossed it aside. He unfastened her lace bra, discarding it before he cupped her breasts with his hands.

His gaze traveled over her. "You're gorgeous, Maddie." He leaned down to take her breast in his mouth, his tongue slowly drawing circles on a taut bud.

She moaned with pleasure, running one hand through his hair, her other hand caressing his body. He was the only man she loved or had ever loved. She had no intention of admitting it to him or openly acknowledging it in any way. Except for Rebecca, who was proof of that love.

Gabe had no idea about her feelings. Gabe was wonderful, but most of his relationships were superficial. He had been superficial with her that summer six years ago.

Now, though she still wasn't sure if he'd changed, nothing he did felt superficial.

He cupped both breasts and drew slow circles with his thumbs.

She moaned again with pleasure, hearing her voice only dimly because her pulse thundered in her ears. She wanted Gabe with all her heart, but when his hands were at her buttons, ready to unfasten her jeans, she gripped his wrists.

"Gabe, wait. This is too fast for me. I can't go back to intimacy with you. It tore me up when we broke up."

He was breathing as hard as she while he gazed at her with half-lidded eyes.

"Maddie, I want you to be mine."

She shook her head. "I'm not a woman who has flings," she said, pulling her clothing in place swiftly, her hands shaking while emotion tore at her. She ached with wanting him, yet giving in was the way to catastrophe. "Especially not with you, someone I loved. You know I was getting serious that summer. I wanted commitment. You didn't. And you're not ready now."

Something flickered in the depths of his eyes. He inhaled deeply.

"You don't know that, Maddie. Maybe I'm ready to settle down. I want you. I want to make love to you all night long. You're not disappearing out of my life this time, like you did before. I know that was my own fault," he added swiftly. "I let you go when I shouldn't have because I wasn't ready for a serious commitment."

"You always knew what I wanted," she whispered.

"We were too young, Maddie. You were just twenty-one."

"Maybe. Maybe not, Gabe."

"I let you go, too, because I thought you'd come back

here. It never occurred to me you would leave the state and stay away."

"You didn't come after me," she said solemnly.

"I promise, that won't happen again."

Startled by his admission, she was momentarily taken aback. "Shh. Don't say that," she whispered. Hoping to get her emotions under control, she walked away from him. "It's late, Gabe. I can stay here alone tonight. You go on home."

"Nope. While you're here, I stay on the sofa. I don't want to worry about you in this big house by yourself."

"Suit yourself."

"Maddie, I want to take you out again tomorrow night."

"I'm having lunch and spending the afternoon with three of my friends in Dallas tomorrow," she replied stiffly, hurting, torn between wanting him and being angry with him about the past.

He walked over to place his hands on her shoulders. "I'll fly you to Dallas in the morning, and we can stay at my condo, which is large enough you'll have plenty of freedom and privacy. I can put a limo at your use."

The tension left her, and she had to laugh. "That is an irresistible proposition. Limo, Dallas condo, private flight—I will accept. One question first, you're not thinking of joining us for lunch are you?"

"Oh, please. You should know me better than that. I'll be at the office. Once we get to Dallas, you won't even know I'm there until dinner."

"Gabe, if you're within a city block, I will know you're there, but thanks. I'll accept your offer."

"Good. Come sit and talk. I'll keep my distance."

"You didn't dance a lot tonight."

"I was waiting on a certain blonde to be free," he said, and she smiled.

Maddie's cell phone rang, a dim sound, but she could hear it and so could Gabe.

"That's my phone. This late at night, I better take the call," she said. She yanked up her jacket to retrieve her cell and walked away to take the call, aware she was disheveled, her mouth still tingling from his kisses.

"Maddie, I'm sorry to call so late," her mother said. "Everything is all right. Rebecca had a nightmare. I put her in my bed, and she had another one. She's crying and wants to talk to you."

Aware of Gabe nearby, who was watching her and listening, Maddie started walking down the hall.

"Put her on the phone." She could hear sniffles. Her heart lurched when she heard Rebecca's high-pitched voice.

"Mommy."

"Sweetie, I love you and everything is all right. Get Grandma to read a story to you. What story would you like tonight?" Maddie smoothed her hair from her face as she talked.

"Come home."

"Honey, I'll be home as quickly as I can. It won't be tonight or tomorrow. Get Grandma to read to you."

"Okay. I love you."

"I love you, too, honey," she said, relieved to hear Rebecca's voice growing calmer. She missed her daughter badly and wanted to hold her close and comfort her. "I miss you oodles and oodles and will come home just as soon as I possibly can. When I do I will read six stories to you. How's that?"

"Good," Rebecca said. "I love you."

"I love you, too, sweetie. Good night."

Tracie came back on the phone, and Maddie talked to her for a few minutes then ended the call. When she turned around, Gabe was waiting. He had pulled on his shirt and buttoned the last two buttons at his waist.

"Who were you talking to, Maddie?"

Four

"Only family, Gabe. Not a guy. There really isn't one in my life."

"How I'd like to fill that void," he said lightly, not pressing her about the call. But she knew Gabe hadn't put it out of his mind and was curious about who she had talked to.

"Let's have a nightcap and talk. It's not that late," he said, draping his arm across her shoulders.

"We do have some cold beer, milk, tea and there's a wine rack filled with bottles that have been here awhile."

"Cold beer sounds fine."

"And I'll have milk. Tell me about the boys who worked on your ranch, and how you got into that," she said. "I don't recall you doing volunteer projects when I was here."

"I didn't. Tony Ryder got involved with the project

and he talked to Jake, who talked to me about helping because I'm the one on the ranch the most. It's through a nonprofit and involves boys who've had a little trouble with the law, but not enough to incarcerate them. The kids have dropped out of school, or have family problems. That type of thing. The organization tries to get help for them, place them on ranches where they can work and be around good people, around animals. It seems to help. Anyway, I volunteered to take two of them—one was thirteen and the other fourteen. The boys stayed with one of our families who live here on the ranch, and that was additional support for them. It worked out well. They're in school now. I keep up with them."

She turned wide eyes on him. "Gabe, I'm truly surprised. I can't imagine you doing this. You're the youngest in your family. You don't know kids."

"It's not that big a deal, Maddie. Those two kids needed some support and guidance, and I could give that easily. I've got the ranch and the time and the money. Neither kid had ever been on a horse. It was kind of funny and pitiful at first, but they took to it. The transformation in them has been awesome. That's one time the word 'awesome' really fits. The guys out here were great. Those boys took to ranch life as if they had been born to it. It was fun to see the changes in them. I got tutors for them in math and reading and their grades have jumped. I have high hopes for both of them. If they get their grades up and keep them up, I'll send them to college."

"I'm impressed," she said, truly meaning it. She stared at him because the Gabe she had left six years ago would not have tied up his life in any such manner.

"They say leopards never change their spots, but I guess leopards do grow up."

He leaned close to her. "Are you accusing me of being shallow and immature?"

She gazed into the bluest eyes she had ever known. "To be truthful, yes. When I left here I sort of thought you were. Not shallow, but a wee bit immature. That particular year, I don't think you would have taken in two boys who needed help," she said carefully, thinking about Gabe and wondering about the depth of the changes in him.

He stared back intently at her. "You are probably right, Maddie," he admitted.

"You always have been honest."

"I guess I had some growing up to do."

"Maybe we all did, Gabe," she added, remembering how she'd had to grow up quickly when she had a baby. If Gabe had helped those two boys and continued to care about them, how much more would he be interested in his own child? Could she forgive Gabe enough for walking out on her to share her daughter with him? Would Gabe forgive her for withholding that he had a daughter?

She ran her hand across her forehead and tried to focus on what he was telling her. She needed to shove aside her questions and think about them later.

"Have you heard one word I've said?" he asked, studying her, looking amused, but also curious.

"I'm sorry, Gabe. It's been a long day and night."

"Anything I can help with?"

"No, but thanks," she said, smiling at him. "I should take my glass of milk and go to bed. Tomorrow will be another busy day. Take one of the bedrooms upstairs and stay out of my hair."

He grinned. "Yes, ma'am," he said, grabbing up a handful of silky locks and running them along his jaw, "but it's going to be a strain."

"Watch out, Gabe, or you'll be staying downstairs again, on the sofa."

As she reached for her glass of milk, Gabe took her wrist to stop her. "Sure you don't want to sit a minute and talk?"

She shook her head. "Sorry. I'm sure. Maybe another time," she said, knowing that most likely there would be no other time. "I'll turn off the lights."

"I'll get them," he said, moving quickly to switch them off. He dropped his arm casually across her shoulders and they checked the doors and the alarm and then climbed the stairs together. How natural it seemed.

He selected the bedroom closest to hers.

"You have your own bathroom. I'll see you in the morning in the kitchen," she said.

"Yes, you will. I'll be more than happy to tuck you in."

"Forget it, Gabe," she snapped.

He laughed, pulling her into his embrace.

"Okay, only a good-night kiss." He kissed away her protest and in no time she had her arms wrapped around him as she kissed him deeply in return, hot kisses that stirred fantasies instead of assuaging desire.

When she stepped away, they were both gasping for breath. "Tomorrow, Gabe." She entered her bedroom and closed her door, setting her glass of milk on a table.

She heard his boots scrape the bare wood floors and then he was gone. He had not closed his door.

Later, she lay in the dark, her thoughts in turmoil.

She had always felt so right about her decision to keep Rebecca a secret. Revealing the truth would have messed up both their lives, at the time, but now—Gabe had changed and she had too.

Becoming a mother and being in the business world had changed her. She was mature enough now to know she wouldn't have to marry Gabe, even if he tried to pressure her into it. And he would try. Gabe had an old-fashioned streak as solid and real as the old-fashioned mansion he had built.

Now she was strong enough in her own right to be able to turn him down. Gabe had faced challenges and grown. And how thrilled he had been over becoming an uncle. To go right out and buy a baby gift, the coming event had to be important to him. To consider sending two boys to college—that had been a reminder of how much he could do for Rebecca. The question persisted— if he helped kids who weren't his, how much more would he care about his own child?

Questions haunted her and drove away sleep.

While she was here, with him, she needed to take a long look, make an assessment.

She wanted to take some time before giving up the secret that would change so many lives. Her mother and grandparents would not want her to reveal the truth to Gabe. It would mean they would have to share Rebecca and lose precious time with her.

And Maddie had to forgive Gabe for walking out that summer. He had never made promises to her about commitment. She had fallen in love; he had not. She'd thought she wasn't carrying a grudge, but maybe she had been. And maybe it was time to forgive him. As for the bigger issue—maybe it was time to tell him about Rebecca.

* * *

The next morning, Gabe moved quietly around the kitchen. As he made breakfast and tried to avoid clattering dishes, he couldn't keep from thinking about her phone calls. He hadn't heard what she'd said last night, only the tone of her voice, but she'd obviously been talking to someone very special.

The Maddie he had known all his life until her move to Florida would have told him who had called. She had always confided her secrets. He was certain that was no longer the case. Far from it. He was certain she didn't want him to know.

At the same time, she had insisted it wasn't a guy. She had said family. He found that difficult to believe, but she had never lied to him before. If not a guy, who was it? He didn't think she had been talking to her mother, grandmother or grandfather, so who? For that matter, if it *had* been a guy, why not tell him?

And if it hadn't been a guy, why was it so private?

Gabe stared out the window without really seeing the yard. He was totally puzzled. The truth hit home that she had a life far away from him and he was no longer any part of it. Why had he always believed she would come back to Texas?

For the first time since her return, he faced the fact that he had always felt their time together really wasn't over. Now, he saw that notion had been a mistake. She had cut all ties, except with the grandfather who visited her instead of her coming back to Texas to visit him. Maddie would leave this time and never return, and she had made it clear that she didn't want Gabe to come to Florida.

There had to be a guy, he thought. The realization made his insides clench. He didn't want another man to be in her life. He knew the feeling was totally ridiculous. He had no claim on Maddie. But he wanted one. The more he thought about marriage and Maddie, the more he wanted it. They fit perfectly—except for her love of Florida and his love of Texas.

Annoyed at his own thoughts, he worked in silence, finally pouring coffee and sitting near the window to wait for her to wake up. He heard a scrape and looked around. Maddie entered the kitchen, and his gloom dissipated.

"Good morning," he said, ensnared. She wore cream-colored slacks and a matching blouse. Her hair was loose, falling over her shoulders in a golden cascade. He wanted to cross the room, wrap her in his embrace and make love.

Instead, he stood rooted to the spot, watching her. He poured chilled orange juice for her, then crossed to her, holding out the drink. But at the last minute, he couldn't resist. He set the drink on the nearby counter and wrapped his arms around her and kissed her.

Each time he held her, she hesitated for a few seconds before returning his kiss passionately. He desired her with an intensity that startled him. He wanted to make love with her for hours. In spite of her fiery kisses, he felt he was light-years away from getting to do so.

Her hair was silky, smelling fresh and clean. She was soft, warm, pliant in his arms. He leaned over her, kissing her deeply, wanting to seduce her, knowing he couldn't get through to her the way he once had. Regret tore at him.

She wriggled away, smoothing her slacks, which were flawless. "We better stick to schedule, Gabe. I have my day booked. Once I arrive in Dallas I have every moment planned. I do need to get there on time."

"Sure. Have some breakfast."

He served her and sat with her, sipping his cup of steaming coffee while she ate toast and drank orange juice.

"Do you have any appointments today?" she asked.

"I have an appointment this morning with Jake, and I'll be at the stockyards later. You like city life. Tonight I'll show you Dallas. You haven't seen it for six years, have you?"

"Actually, no."

"Great. I'll make dinner reservations."

He pulled a key out of his pocket. "Here's a key to my condo. When we get to Dallas, I'll have the limo drop me at my office. It will take you where you want to go for the rest of the day, and we can meet at my condo in time for dinner. How's that?"

"Sounds grand," she said, flashing a warm smile that made him anticipate the evening.

His hand brushed hers as she took the key and slipped it into her pocket. Quickly, she finished her breakfast. Excusing herself and stepping to the window, she called Sol to tell him her plans.

Gabe could easily hear her. She made no effort to speak softly. Whoever she had talked to in Florida, the person had been far more important to her than Sol, and Sol was a lifelong employee and friend. The puzzle grew, and Gabe was at more of a loss than ever.

"I can be ready in ten minutes, Gabe. Is that too soon to leave?"

"Not at all," he replied, pulling out his cell phone. "My pilot already has an approximate time for our departure. I'll let him know."

She rinsed her dishes and placed them in the

dishwasher alongside Gabe's. She hurried out of the kitchen and was gone.

He stared after her, realizing just how big the changes in her were. She had moved on. He shouldn't expect her to pick up where they'd left off, but somehow he *had* expected the same close friendship they'd once shared, even if they were not lovers. Growing up, she had always shadowed him, done whatever he was doing, kept in constant touch with him. That sharing seemed to be over. The changes in her shouldn't continue to surprise him, but they did.

From the moment he had recognized her on the side of the road, she had been one surprise after another. So many unexpected differences now. She was more poised, confident, and didn't need him the way she used to.

He got ready to go and waited for her at the back door. She entered the room, her long blond hair swinging gently across her shoulders with each step.

He watched while she set the alarm, and then they left.

They chatted through the drive to the airport and then on board the family jet. He had taken women on the jet half a dozen times before, and they had always been impressed with the private plane, even women who came from families that owned their own planes. It was plush, with an elegant interior. He noticed Maddie paid little attention to it, making him wonder about her own lifestyle and how accustomed she was to luxury and to flying.

"Maddie, I want you to visit Texas again," he said, leaning closer, putting his elbows on his knees. Her skin was flawless. He could look at her all day. Her beauty took his breath.

She smiled, looking cool and reserved, and he knew what her answer would be before she shook her head.

"Gabe, I told you, I don't plan to return anytime soon. I have a busy life."

"I can't believe you're that wrapped up in your work. There's no man?"

"Absolutely not. And it's not all work. I'm wrapped up in my life there. I have family, friends."

"Your mom doesn't miss Texas?"

"Actually, she does. Mom's two lifetime best friends are in Dallas. She visits them several times a year, and she would see Granddad while she was here. She'll keep seeing them."

"Maybe I ought to call and prevail on her to bring you along."

"I've outgrown that. I doubt if you will miss me much or often. We're almost strangers now."

He reached up to touch her silky hair. "Strangers with you? Not ever. I know so much about you, Maddie, as you do about me. For years we were friends and then it became much, much more," he said, his voice dropping in timbre as he looked into her wide, brown eyes. Her lips parted, and she drew a deep breath. He wanted to slip the pale buttons free of her blouse and pull her onto his lap. "I know so much about you. I know how you look in passionate moments—"

"Gabe, I walked into that one. So, okay, we still know each other," she said, gulping for air and obviously trying to make her voice firm. "No, I won't be back, and, no, you won't miss me," she said, surprising him with the note of steel in her reply. "I have a life. It's over a thousand miles away and does not involve you. You've been fine with that for the past six years so don't tell me it's different now."

He caught her chin in his hand and slipped his other arm around her waist suddenly, turning her to look into his eyes. "Then why does your heart pound when I touch you? Why are you breathless? Why are your kisses hot? Why do you cling to me when I kiss you?" he demanded.

He could see anger flash in her eyes. Was she upset that he could see so easily the effect he had on her? When her lips parted, he moved his head to close the last inch between them. He placed his mouth on hers as he kissed her.

She responded, kissing him in return, and he flipped free her seat belt and lifted her to his lap, holding her against him as he continued to kiss her.

When she finally broke away and slipped back to her seat, she buckled up, looking shaken. With a lift to her shoulders, she raised her head to look him straight in the eye.

"So I'm physically attracted to you. I'm vulnerable because I haven't been kissed in a long time. I can't resist you physically. But it's only attraction, Gabe. It's meaningless, so don't put stock in my response to you. I mean what I say about leaving Texas."

"And I mean what I say about getting you to stay longer," he said, leaning close again. "I want to make love with you, Maddie."

"It's not going to happen," she whispered. "Where's the lavatory?"

He pointed, telling her. He watched as she walked away, her hips swaying slightly. She was holding back. He had known her too well and for too long. There was something she wasn't telling him. Whatever it was, it was tied to those phone calls she had taken.

She was gone a long time. When she returned, she

looked composed. For the remainder of the flight she managed to keep their conversation turning constantly to impersonal topics.

In Dallas, they took a limo to the headquarters of the Benton family business. Gabe brushed her cheek with a light kiss and climbed out. "See you tonight," he said, closing the door.

He watched the limo drive away and then entered the office building, already thinking about the evening and where he would make reservations for dinner. It was Saturday. She hadn't settled on an agency yet to handle selling the ranch, which meant she would be here at least through next week. He hoped longer. He wanted to change her mind about coming back to Texas for a visit. He wanted to change her mind about inviting him to Florida. Most of all, he wanted to change her mind about making love. She set him ablaze. Right now, he wanted to be with her and he had a feeling he wouldn't be able to concentrate on anything else.

Maddie spent the morning shopping for gifts to take to Rebecca, to her mother and to her grandparents. She met her friends for lunch, which extended into a long afternoon. At half-past four, the group broke up and she took the limo back to Gabe's condo.

She called him on her cell phone and learned he would be there within the hour.

Using his key, she let herself in and dropped her purchases on a sofa. She walked through the elegant condo that looked untouched. How much time did Gabe actually spend here? Someone probably cleaned for him—often. The hardwood floors gleamed and the dark mahogany furniture held the faint scent of furniture polish. Thick area rugs in deep blues were in various living areas. The view of Dallas would be spectacular at night. She touched the piano, wondering why he had one. She knew he didn't play a note. She paused at the door of the master bedroom and then roamed around inside. There were a few pictures of Gabe with his brother and his deceased sister, Brittany. There was a picture of Jake, Gabe and Caitlin Santerre, now Caitlin Benton. Maddie had known Caitlin as far back as she could remember because they had gone to school together.

She glanced at the big bed, wondering about Gabe and the women who had been in his life. She was certain there had been women. Gabe was a fun-loving man who liked women, and they liked him.

Maddie left the room, examining each bedroom and finally picking the one the farthest from Gabe's. After gathering her purchases and carrying them to the bedroom she had chosen, she closed the door. All day she had avoided thinking about Gabe and Rebecca. She would finish her business here and get back to Florida before disaster befell her. She could stop worrying about whether or not she was doing the right thing, or trying to figure out if Gabe had changed and matured.

She should take this evening and enjoy him. But could she do that and not tell him about Rebecca? If she could, then she'd be on her way back home to Florida with her heart intact and her family at peace. Gabe would never know.

It wasn't that simple. Not after all she had learned about Gabe since being home. He had changed.

Yet when she even speculated about telling Gabe the truth, her insides knotted. He was a take-charge person, a man of action. Once she revealed the truth, there would be no turning back.

Gabe was arrogant. He could have a dig-in-your-heels

attitude. His wishes might not coincide with hers at all. If she revealed the truth to him, she had to be sure that was what she wanted. It would tie her life with Gabe's forever. Was that what she really wanted?

On the other hand, if Gabe had truly changed, grown more responsible, more interested in kids, didn't Rebecca deserve to know her father? He was a wonderful man. And Gabe deserved to know his daughter.

Who knew what Gabe would want to do? And once he decided, he'd never let up. He had far more wealth than she did. There was no way she could fight him in court or any other way. He had the money, the time, the contacts.

She sat on a chair by a window and called home, getting her mother first and then Rebecca. When she ended the call, she gazed out the window without seeing anything, simply thinking about telling Gabe the truth. She didn't want to. Yet each time she thought about returning to Florida without him knowing, she didn't feel right.

She thought about the pregnancy and childbirth she had gone through when she had been twenty-one. During that time, she had wanted Gabe with all her heart. The most joyous moments in her life had also been bitter, because Gabe had walked out on her that summer.

More questions came instead of easy solutions. If she told Gabe about Rebecca, Maddie faced another formidable question. Could she bear to watch him marry someone else while their lives were intertwined? No matter how hot the attraction, she and Gabe could never make a relationship work, because she wouldn't leave Florida and he wouldn't leave Texas. Gabe wasn't the type to settle for a long-distance marriage. So he would marry. He had already mentioned settling down and he was building his home. Then she would have to cooperate with Gabe and his wife. That situation would hurt. Gabe was the only man she had ever loved. She suspected that would be true for the rest of her life.

She still hesitated to reveal Rebecca because it would mean huge changes in her life, along with upheaval in her family's lives. Changes that would be far-reaching and permanent. It would mean countless trips between Texas and Florida. There would be no leaving Texas behind forever. No matter what happened between her and Gabe during this current trip, revealing the truth would mean her life would be connected to Gabe's irrevocably. She wasn't sure she wanted to deal with that.

Thinking of the possibilities, asking herself the tough questions, Maddie frowned as she struggled for decisions.

"Tell him," she whispered to the empty room, knowing she would have to, yet still dreading it. Taking a deep breath, she walked toward the closed door while arguments battled silently within her.

Yet she kept coming back to one fact. Rebecca had a right to know her father, who would love her.

Gabe and Rebecca both deserved the truth.

Filled with dread, she got ready to shower and change.

When she finally emerged from the shower, she had a towel wrapped around herself and she had blow-dried her hair.

As she crossed to the boxes she had placed on the bed, there was a knock on the door.

"I'm not dressed."

"Can I come in anyway?" Gabe called, opening the door a crack. "Are you presentable?" he asked while he was still out of sight.

"Not really. I'm in a towel."

"Hey, great," he said, opening the door and stepping inside. He held a dozen red roses in a crystal vase. "I brought these for you."

"They're beautiful and should last far beyond the next few minutes." She smiled. "Do you understand 'not dressed' and I'm 'not presentable'?"

He paused to let his gaze roam slowly over her. "I understand, but you're wrong. You're absolutely, gorgeously presentable, and you're covered more than you would be on the beach or at the pool. Which, speaking of, want to swim?"

"Thank you, I'll pass."

He set down the flowers and walked over to place his hands on her bare shoulders. The contact sent streams of fire through her insides.

"Gabe, I'll see you in a little while."

"One kiss while I can hold you close, with only a towel between us," he said softly. His husky voice set her pulse racing as he wrapped her in his arms and kissed her.

She shouldn't, yet how to resist him? Resistance was impossible when it was Gabe. She wanted to toss aside wisdom and caution and kiss him in return. She wanted to let go and for one brief moment, she did, relishing the feel of him against her. She ached to forget everything and drop the towel, but instead, she stepped away.

"Now you have to go," she whispered, unable to find her voice. Her heart pounded. She wanted him with an intensity that shook her.

She didn't want to leave Texas with her heart in knots

once again over Gabe. And she didn't want to rekindle anything between them. If she had to tell him about Rebecca, then it was imperative to have distance between them so she could keep her wits about her. Once he knew the truth, Gabe would come after her with marriage on his mind, no matter what he felt in his heart. He hadn't changed that much in all the years.

"I have to dress, Gabe. I'll see you in about half an hour."

His heated gaze raked over her again, making her tingle as if his fingers had drifted over her. He was aroused, studying her intently, standing with his fists clenched.

"You don't know what you do to me, Maddie," he said in a deep, hoarse voice.

"There was a time when I would have melted had I heard you say that," she admitted. "But not any longer, Gabe. That time is gone. I'll see you shortly for dinner."

They stood in tense silence, their gazes locked. Desire flamed in the depths of his eyes. She felt hot, tingling, wanting him beyond anything she had thought possible. Yet she stood rooted to the floor, resisting what her body clamored to have.

He turned and was gone, closing the door behind him.

She sagged and gulped deep breaths. Longing shook her.

She'd resolved to tell him the truth about his child. Now she would have to find the right moment to do so.

Five

Gabe showered and dressed in a charcoal suit with a white shirt and red tie. Gold cuff links gleamed in his French cuffs. With mounting anticipation, he waited in the living area of the condo, gazing at the city spread below.

When Maddie entered the room, his heart missed beats. In a simple red, sleeveless dress that ended above her knees, she crossed the room. Her blond hair was caught up on her head and pinned, hanging loosely in back. The vee neck of the dress revealed luscious curves and her long, shapely legs were as gorgeous as he remembered.

Drawn to her, he approached. "You look stunning," he said in a husky voice. Big brown eyes held his gaze, and her full lips were an invitation. He could sit and look at her all evening long.

"Thank you. You look quite handsome yourself," she

said in a subdued voice, and he focused more intently on her.

She looked stunning, composed and poised, yet he had the feeling something was dreadfully wrong. Maddie wasn't the open book she used to be. She no longer shared her life. Not any of it, least of all her concerns. He couldn't shake the feeling there was something he had missed and the feeling strengthened as he faced her.

"Ready for an evening out in a dazzling city?"

She gave him a glorious smile that almost made him think he was making a mistake about her feelings. "Ever so eager to see the sights," she replied lightly.

He walked up to wrap his arms around her. "I want you, Maddie. More than ever."

She shook her head. "Don't, Gabe. No matter how I may feel about you, there's no future between us. I love Miami as much as you love the ranch. That says it all."

He inhaled deeply. "I want you anyway. We can make love with no thought of tomorrow or Texas or Florida."

"That sounds like the Gabe I know," she said, smiling at him and stepping away. "One of us will cling to reason and logic. Now, I'm ready for this night on the town."

He took her arm, and they left, going to the waiting limo.

Gabe took her to a private club high above the city. The place suited him tonight, with its candlelight, roses on linen-covered tables and a combo playing old ballads as a few couples moved about a small dance floor. Adding to the ambiance, the view of the city was spectacular. Lights twinkled, and in the far western sky, the last rose streaks of sunset splashed across a darkening horizon.

As soon as they were seated at a table by a floor-to-ceiling window, Gabe ordered drinks and stood to take her hand. "Let's dance, Maddie."

When she walked into his arms, he drew her close, dancing to a ballad he knew she liked. She smelled like roses and lilacs, and she was soft and warm in his embrace. The dress was a thin barrier. He ached to make love to her. And he wished he knew how to get her to tell him what worries she had. He hoped she had meant what she said. Once upon a time, he wouldn't have questioned whether or not she meant what she said.

"Maddie, what's worrying you?" he asked quietly. "You used to share your joys and concerns with me."

She gazed at him with eyes that told him nothing about her feelings. "I have things back home on my mind, Gabe. I have never been away from work for long. I can do a few things long-distance, but not much. I'd like to wind up the business with the ranch and get that behind me. I had another talk with an agency this morning. I think I've decided to go with the one you suggested. Mr. Trockburn has been helpful."

"Ed's a hard worker and efficient. He'll do a good job for you."

"I think so. He's coming to the ranch Monday morning."

"Is that all?" he asked, searching her face for some clue, wishing she would share everything with him the way she used to do.

"Yes. Since when did you start worrying about me?" she asked too sharply, making him wonder if she had truly forgiven him for walking out. "You haven't known the problems I've faced over these past six years," she added.

"No," he answered. "I'm beginning to regret more

and more about the past, and that's one of the things I wish I could change. I want you in my life now, Maddie. I really do," he said, meaning it with all his heart.

"Don't be silly, Gabe. That's your physical reaction talking. You weren't thinking about me while we were separated, so it's ridiculous to look back over it in regret now. We both made our choices."

"Doesn't mean I might not regret some of the ones I made."

The music ended and a faster number played. She began to dance, smiling at him with an inscrutable look. Tantalized, he wanted her more than ever. He danced with her, both of them moving fast, her hips swaying.

He could feel beads of sweat on his forehead, but he didn't think it was from dancing. It was from watching Maddie. She was a flame, sexy and taunting. She slanted him a hot look, filled with temptation. She was flirting with him now, with her sultry glances, her sensuous moves. He had to control the urge to yank her into his embrace and kiss her.

He unbuttoned his coat, moving around her. When the number ended, he caught her, spinning her around and dipping her low. She wrapped her arms around him as she looked up into his eyes.

Their gazes locked as he raised her slowly. If he could, he would take her out of here right now, back to his condo and into his bed. He knew she would not consent, so he didn't attempt anything. She stood facing him, their gazes still holding. He drew her to him. Only inches away, she stopped.

Another ballad started and wordlessly they began to dance. She followed his lead, moving into his embrace. They were in perfect rhythm, falling into patterns they had practiced so many times through the years.

She was light as a feather and followed his lead perfectly. He knew so much about her and also so little. In some ways, she might as well be a stranger he had just met. In other ways, she was closer to him than any woman had ever been.

When the music ended, he took her hand. "Let's sit out a few." At their table he held her chair, letting his fingers drift across her nape and brush her shoulder lightly.

Gabe sat facing her. As they sipped their glasses of wine, several times she caught him studying her intently. He knew her too well. His questions indicated he sensed something amiss in her life, and knowing Gabe, he perceived it included him. He had always been sensitive to her feelings. She'd been right to have assumed he would still be that way.

It used to make her feel close to him. Now it disturbed her that he could read her so well. Once again, urgency tugged at her. She needed to tell him about Rebecca. But it had to be the right moment. She suspected when she told him everything, it would change how he felt about her. He might not forgive her. It might mean the end of her friendship with him.

He still made her heart pound just looking at him. He looked incredibly handsome. Always appealing to her, he was even more so in the charcoal suit with his impeccable white monogrammed shirt and gold cuff links. He looked what he was—a multimillionaire filled with self-confidence and a zest for life.

Tonight, there was a sober side to him, but she suspected it was because he thought something was bothering her.

She wished she could stop thinking about their

situation for the night. She longed to relax and enjoy being with Gabe. But it was impossible to turn off one of the most pressing problems she had ever had.

It was difficult to keep her mind on Gabe's conversation, but she tried to concentrate. If he realized how worried she really was, he wouldn't let up until he got some kind of answer.

"Maddie, dammit. What the hell is bothering you?" Gabe asked quietly.

She blinked and realized she had been so wrapped in her thoughts she hadn't heard a word he had said.

"Sorry, Gabe. I really am having a great time. Selling the ranch is pressing, and I got lost in my thoughts about it."

"I think it's more than that. You'll sell the ranch."

She smiled at him, trying to push her dilemma out of her mind and concentrate on giving all her attention to Gabe. "You're right. I shouldn't worry about the sale."

"You used to share every little joy and sorrow with me, and I guess I still expect you to do that. It worries me when you don't. Old habits are hard to break."

"Maybe you're too much of a take-charge person for me to share my worries with tonight. You'd step in and rearrange my life."

He held his wineglass and studied her. "I couldn't possibly step in and rearrange your life unless you asked me to," he said, and she wished she could take back her words. She could see Gabe mulling over what she had told him.

"Here comes our waiter to take our order."

After they had ordered, Gabe stood and came around to hold her chair. "Dancing is always good. I can hold you and it helps to move around and work off steam."

To her relief, it was a fast number and it did help to

move and stop thinking for a few minutes. She wanted to be in his arms, wanted to kiss him. She had fought this attraction since he had pulled her into his embrace to kiss her their first night together, but she wanted to make love with him. Just one more time. She was already in love with him. Making love would not change her feelings for him. But after she told him the truth, everything else *would* change.

She danced around him, watching him, seeing her desire mirrored in his eyes. He wanted her, there was no question or doubt. He had made that clear since that first moment on the highway.

Brushing against him, she circled him. His blue eyes flamed with blatant lust. Some locks of her hair fell free, and she shook them from her face.

Gabe reached out to take her wrist, turning her then holding her hand as they danced. He pulled her close for another dip that left her clinging to him, gazing into his eyes and thinking about kissing him.

The music ended and he slowly raised her up. He wanted to kiss, and she did, too, but they were in a public place. She didn't want to make a spectacle. She turned to walk back to their table, but a ballad started and Gabe drew her into his embrace, holding her close to his heated body.

"You're hot."

"Not half as hot as you are," he said, giving the word a whole different meaning. "You burn me to ashes by dancing around me, tempting me, teasing me."

"I didn't hear a protest at the time."

"Never a protest. I want you alone with me. I want to peel you out of that red dress and kiss you until you're as on fire as I am," he whispered in her ear. Her heartbeat raced, and she wondered if he could feel it.

"Kiss you all over. From your head to your toes. Slowly," he continued, barely moving, his warm breath tickling her ear as he whispered to her.

"Stop trying to seduce me," she said, twisting to look up at him.

"I think you want the same thing I do. You dance as if you do. Your eyes are filled with desire. Your body language says loving is what you want."

"So you're right. That doesn't mean it will happen."

He placed one hand on her cheek. "I'm going to love you, Maddie. We'll make love together, I promise you, before you try to walk out of my life again. I'm going to tie your heart to mine so you won't want to say goodbye."

She drew in a deep breath. His words thrilled her. She couldn't help but respond to the note of steel in his voice. Revealing the truth about Rebecca would forever change her relationship with Gabe. She wanted this one night with him. One night of loving Gabe and being loved by him. Before she confessed, she wanted a memory she could hold forever.

He took his hand from her cheek.

"Gabe, you know I want the same thing you do, but it makes parting hurt more." Even as she spoke, she thought of Rebecca. Maddie had a future with Gabe, but not one filled with love and shared joys.

"There's no way we can predict what the future holds."

The music ended and Gabe took her hand. "Our dinners are served. I saw the server stop at our table."

When they sat to eat, Gabe barely touched his dinner while he talked to her. She ate a thick, juicy steak that was delicious.

"I don't eat as much beef in Florida as I do seafood,

but here, the steaks are wonderful," she said, thinking more about Gabe's blue eyes than about her dinner. "You haven't eaten much of yours."

"I'm hungry for something else," he drawled.

She sipped her water, gazing over the rim of her glass at him, knowing both of them were thinking about hot kisses and making love.

Her cell phone rang and when she stood, Gabe came to his feet.

"Sorry, Gabe. I need to take this call. I'll be back." She fished out her cell phone and left, trying to put some distance between them before she answered the call from home.

When she finished talking to Rebecca, she left the lobby and returned to the table. Gabe had eaten a little more of his dinner.

She kept the conversation impersonal while they finished their meal and then they returned to dancing. An hour later, when the musicians took a break, Gabe took her arm. "Let's go somewhere else. I told you I'd show you Dallas."

"You have. The views here and at your condo are spectacular. I saw a lot today. I shopped and bought this dress for tonight."

"You did well. It's gorgeous. I've told you what I think about it. Or have you forgotten?"

"Yes, you've told me, and no, I haven't forgotten. That wouldn't be possible." Since she would have only one night with him, she wanted it to last. She hoped to draw it out and make each moment a memory that she could hold forever.

They left the club, and he drove to another one. Before he stepped out of the car, he shed his coat and tie and unbuttoned the top button of his shirt. "Put your purse in the trunk. You won't hear your cell phone anyway."

She did as he asked and walked with him toward the entrance. Lights glittered on the outside, and a flashing neon arrow pointed downstairs to a basement area where the rock beat blared loud and fast.

The place was dark, packed, with strobe lights blinking. She laughed when they danced. He looked at her quizzically.

"What?" he shouted above the deafening music.

"You. Here," she shouted back, dancing around him. "The cowboy—not your usual."

As he grinned, he unfastened more buttons of his shirt. She removed the remaining pins from her hair, letting it fall free while she gyrated to the heavy beat. The music prohibited conversation.

It was sexy and fun to dance wildly, to let go and forget everything else. Gabe was too appealing, locks of his brown hair falling across his forehead. With his shirt unbuttoned and his steamy moves, he wove a web of seduction. Even in his fancy black Western boots, he was a dream dancer, light on his feet, his obvious enjoyment contagious.

One piece led into another without pause, and she lost all sense of time.

Finally, Gabe took her hand and jerked his head toward the door. She followed him as they threaded through the crowd and then stepped into cool, fresh air.

She laughed. "That was exhilarating."

"We can go back to the club, drive around and take in the city then get a nightcap or go to my condo."

"I'll opt for the last choice," she said.

"What I wanted exactly," he said with obvious

satisfaction as he held the car door for her to climb inside.

They arrived at his condo and she settled for her usual nighttime drink of milk while Gabe had a cold beer. They had a balcony with a spectacular view and the evening air had cooled. A faint breeze made the balcony even more comfortable.

Gabe pulled his chair close to hers, holding her hand while they reminisced.

"Will you take anything back to Florida from your childhood home?" he asked.

"Sure. I've been packing boxes. I'll have them shipped. It's expensive, but not as costly as driving here and back to get them. There's no furniture that I want. Mom took the few things that I would have been interested in." While she talked, Gabe released her hand to play with strands of her hair. She tingled with awareness of his touch.

They continued talking about incidental things and events, local people and what they were doing, but she was more aware of Gabe's fingers brushing her shoulder and nape, turning locks of her hair in his hand. His white shirt was still open by several buttons, revealing glimpses of his muscled chest and brown chest curls. He was incredibly handsome, more so now than when they were younger. She looked at his mouth, remembering his kisses, wanting to kiss him now.

"Do you have any furniture from your family home?" she asked.

"Actually, I do. When Jake made the deal with Dad about the house, Mom asked me to pick out what I would really like to have and talk to Jake about what was agreeable with him. There really was not that much I wanted, so it worked out fine."

"You'll live on the ranch, go out with local ladies, marry one and settle for ranch life forever," she said, unable to resist combing stray locks of brown hair off his forehead simply because she wanted to touch him.

Gabe leaned close and picked her up, swiftly lifting her to place her in his lap. "Maddie, I want you in my future."

Her protest died when she looked into Gabe's eyes. They conveyed his desire. Her mouth opened, but words failed her. Then he covered her mouth with his.

Her heart thudded. Winding her arms around his neck, she kissed him while she tossed aside worries. She would take this night with Gabe. She would pour out her love. One night with the man she had always loved.

One night before she finally told him the truth.

<u>Six</u>

Maddie's heart pounded while she kissed Gabe passionately. Just tonight, she had told herself while dancing. Only once to show him how much she loved him, to rediscover and store up a memory that she could hold forever.

It had only been since she'd returned to Texas that she had faced the fact that she didn't think she could ever love anyone except Gabe. In the six years she'd been away from him, she hadn't realized that she still loved him. She had always reassured herself she was over him, her memories had faded and she didn't care. During that time, no other man had ever really appealed to her. With his first kiss, six long years of trying to forget Gabe crumbled into nonexistence. She had to face the truth.

He was the sole love of her life.

Tomorrow, she would tell him about his child. Gabe

took family seriously. He was close to Jake and had been close to his sister, Brittany. He was close to his parents. When he learned he had a daughter born five years ago, he might not forgive her for keeping Rebecca's birth a secret.

No matter her good intentions, fathers had rights, and she had violated Gabe's. He might not understand why she'd done it. Gabe had an old-fashioned streak in him and it showed up in all aspects of his life. There was a chance he would be angry, bitter and unforgiving about Rebecca.

Tonight was the time to make love with him, if ever. To love and be loved again by the one man who truly owned her heart.

She kissed him passionately, wanting this night to be the most memorable of all.

Gabe cradled her against his shoulder while his kisses scalded her and made her want more.

"We're outside. This balcony is public."

"Not really," he said, lifting her easily as he stood. "But we'll go inside," he said, and returned to kissing her. She paid no attention to where he carried her until he set her on her feet near a bed.

He never stopped kissing her, only now his hands were free. He caressed her. His hands roamed over her, down her back and over her bottom, his other hand on her hip, moving lower to her thigh.

He found the zipper to her dress and pulled it down enough to slip the top off. It fell to her waist, and she slipped her arms out of it while they continued to kiss.

Gabe's kisses set her ablaze. How much she loved him!

He held her away from him so he could look at her. As soon as he flipped free the catch to the wisp of a bra she wore, he cupped her breasts with his hands, his thumbs drawing lazy circles on her nipples. "You are beautiful, Maddie. So beautiful. More than you used to be." He pushed away the dress, letting it fall to the floor with a whisper of cool air on her ankles.

Holding his arms, she closed her eyes while sensations rocked her. She opened her eyes to finish unbuttoning his shirt and tug it out of his pants. In seconds, she pushed it away, letting it fall unheeded to the floor.

Holding his narrow waist, she ran one hand over his bare, muscled chest, tangling her fingers in his chest hair. She moaned with pleasure from his caresses and kisses.

"You're gorgeous," he whispered thickly. He leaned down to kiss her, taking one breast in his mouth, his tongue circling where his thumb had been. "Maddie, how I've dreamed about this. How I've wanted you! You can't ever know how much I've wanted you. I want you here in my bed. In my arms. I don't want you to leave. I want you to stay here with me."

"That won't happen," she whispered, wondering if he even heard what she said to him.

"You don't know what you do to me." He showered kisses on her temple, down to her throat, then to her ear.

His deep breath made his chest expand. She stood in low cut, lace panties and no stockings, because of the summer weather.

He peeled down her panties, and she stepped out of them.

"You're totally gorgeous. The most beautiful woman on earth. Maddie," he said, longing in his expression as he enveloped her in his embrace and kissed her passionately.

She unfastened and pulled away his belt. Then her fingers went to his trousers, which soon fell around his feet. He kicked them away. She gasped for breath, taking in the sight of him. He was tall, strong, aroused. Ready for her. She ran her hands across his broad shoulders, feeling the taut muscles, relishing the hardness, the strength of him.

"You make me melt to look at you," she whispered.

She clung to him, only his briefs between them. He was warm, hard, muscled. His body was perfection and she was on fire with wanting him to love her. She peeled away his briefs, freeing him, running her hands over his hips and along his thighs, then up again to wrap her arms around his neck.

"I'm the one on fire from looking. I've dreamed of this moment. Six years ago you were a beautiful girl. Now you're a breathtaking woman, all grown up, perfection. It's dazzling to look at you, Maddie."

"It's been so long," she said.

"I told you I wanted to kiss you from head to toe," he whispered in her ear. He picked her up, pausing to sweep back the covers before placing her on the bed. Then he knelt beside her, pushing her down gently and turning her onto her belly.

He began at her feet and left slow, hot kisses up over her calves and the backs of her thighs, taking his time, a sweet torment that increased her tension and made her want him more than ever.

Digging her fingers into the bed, she relished his touches. It was reality and not a dream. She was with Gabe. Gabe kissing her. Gabe caressing her. Gabe making her melt. She couldn't get enough, and she couldn't stop feeling as if it were a dream she would wake from.

Looking over her shoulder at him, she saw that his blue eyes had darkened with desire and his gaze was hot, intense. Each kiss added to the storm that swept her. She already ached for him, wanting to be one with him if only for tonight.

His hands played over her bottom as he roamed higher. His hands and hot breath were at the juncture at the back of her thighs, and she opened her legs to give him access.

When she moaned softly and attempted to roll over, he pushed her against the bed and continued kissing her back and nape. She rolled over, looking up into his eyes, which held consuming desire.

Scooping her into his arms, he kissed her. She returned his kiss while rubbing her body lightly against his. Their kisses muffled his moan.

"This is the way it should be, Maddie. You belong in my arms. Your heart belongs to me and always has."

"Shh. Take tonight. It's what we have," she said, trying to avoid giving credence to what he said, words that thrilled her even when she couldn't believe them.

He caught one hand in her hair while his other arm banded her waist. "It doesn't have to be just tonight. It doesn't at all, Maddie. That's your choice."

She pulled him close, trying to win his heart with hot kisses that he couldn't resist.

"You'll miss me. I'm part of your life. Just as you're part of mine now, and forever."

As she kissed him and ended his words, he held her tightly. She could feel his pounding heart against her own. While she ran her hands over his chest, she continued kissing him.

"I've missed you, badly," she whispered, knowing she shouldn't admit her feelings to him but unable to hold back the words. She showered kisses over his face and throat, feeling his faint beard stubble. Her hands ran across his shoulders and down his smooth, muscled back. She couldn't get enough of him. And then, as if he had the same thought about her, he pushed her down on the bed and started again at her feet. Working his way up with a tantalizing slowness, so deliberate, he watched her while she watched him in return, trying to resist grabbing him and kissing him.

His brown hair was a tangle now, locks falling over his forehead. He still looked powerful, sexy, appealing. His hands were a torment, caressing her as he moved up her inner thighs until she opened her legs to give him access.

Then she was lost in sensation. He trailed kisses over her breasts while his hands played between her legs and she spread them wider for him.

"Gabe, I want you," she whispered, pulling him to her.

He kissed her, silencing her words.

She sat up to kiss and caress him as he had her. She stroked him, letting her tongue run freely over him to pleasure him in every way.

She relished rediscovery. She wanted to create a night he would remember. This was transient, a shared moment that would not happen again, and she wanted it to be all it could possibly be for him, because it already was for her.

"Gabe," she breathed, suddenly, sitting up and framing his face with her hands to kiss him deeply, passionately.

He crushed her close in his embrace, and she could feel his heart racing as hers was.

She moved astride him, fondling him. As she ran her hands over him, she committed the feel of him to memory, pouring out her love for him.

With a growl deep in his throat, he swung her onto her back and moved between her legs to begin loving her all over again, his hands and mouth giving her pleasure.

Desire built with each touch and kiss until she was gasping, on fire with need.

His breath was as ragged as hers.

"Gabe," she whispered. "I'm not protected."

He stepped off the bed and crossed the room to pick up his trousers and get a packet from his billfold. He removed it and returned. She climbed out of bed to meet him, wrapping her arms around him when they kissed.

Lifting her to the bed, he knelt between her legs.

She watched while he put on the condom. He came down to kiss her, keeping his weight from settling fully on her.

He entered her slowly, teasing and making her arch against him. Her hips thrust and she ran her hands on his hard bottom and muscled thighs. He slowly filled her, withdrawing and entering again. Crying out with pleasure, she thrashed beneath him.

"I want you now." She held him tightly, her long legs locked around him. He eased into her again and then moved slowly, building the tension. When sensations rocked her, he kept iron control. Sweat beaded his shoulders and chest. She moved wildly, clinging to him.

"Gabe, now," she whispered.

The roaring of her own pulse drowned out any other

noise. She tugged at him while he drew out the loving as long as possible.

Finally, he lost control, groaning deeply when he thrust hard and fast and she moved with him. They rocked together, pleasure soaring. As they burst over a brink, he shuddered with his release and rapture enveloped her.

She gasped for breath while waves of ecstasy rocked her. "Ah, Gabe."

"Maddie, you're perfection," he whispered hoarsely. Even as his thrusts slowed, she clung to him.

"I've wanted that since you stood on the road and told me hello," he gasped. "Can you stay in bed with me tomorrow?"

She laughed. "That's a question I never expected to hear. We plan a whole day in bed—"

"Most definitely," he replied. "The whole day and tomorrow night, too. Ranch or here, I don't care, but if here, we don't have to dress and go out at all."

"That's ridiculous," she whispered, in euphoria, refusing to think about anything except enjoying how she felt and remembering the past few minutes.

For now, she was in Gabe's arms, one with him, in paradise. This was perfection, and she didn't want to think beyond this moment with him.

She brushed damp locks of hair back from his forehead while he did the same for her.

"You're beautiful. You take my breath away," he said.

"You definitely take mine, you handsome man," she said lightly.

He rolled on his side, taking her with him and holding her close. He smiled at her. "This is the best. This is the way it was meant to be and more. So much more." He showered kisses on her temple, down to her ear and then on her throat. "Ah, Maddie, I can't tell you how great it is to make love, to hold you in my arms, to have you here close to my heart."

Wonderful words, but not the ones she had always wished he would say, although now she didn't feel so strongly about wanting to hear them because it wouldn't matter whether they loved each other or not. Their lifestyles were set and neither wanted to change. She could no more give up her life than Gabe could give up his precious ranch.

He raised up on an elbow. "Will you?"

She laughed as she caressed his jaw, sliding her hand down to his chest to tangle her fingers in the mat of curls. "Will I what?"

"Stay here tomorrow with me?"

She sighed. "Don't intrude with talk about tomorrow just yet. We'll talk in the morning."

"Deal," he said, smiling. "I want to make you want to come back to Texas. Your roots are here. I'm here."

She placed her finger on his lips. "If you want me to stay tomorrow, you'll stop right now with the arguments."

"What arguments? I've spent the most fantastic— Hour? Two hours? I have no idea how much time, but it was fabulous. I want to hold you close and kiss you a little and touch you a lot."

She laughed as he wrapped an arm around her, smiling at her with satisfaction.

"I'll never forget this night, Maddie. It was magic."

"I quite agree and I don't want the world to intrude in any way." She paused, suddenly overwhelmed by emotion. "Gabe, forgive me when I disappoint you."

He smiled. "You won't disappoint me and I'll always—"

"Just remember I asked you to forgive me," she whispered, placing her fingers on his lips and stopping his words. "We go way back, and we've been through a lot together."

"True. Remember when I taught you to ride your new bicycle?"

"My dad was involved with the ranch and kept putting off teaching me."

"You were cute and bright and did what I told you. I felt sorry for you after catching you crying when you crashed on your new bike, smashing a bed of your mom's flowers. I thought you'd kill your bike before you learned to ride it."

She smiled. "You got me out of a lot of scrapes."

"Show me your gratitude," he said in a husky voice.

She smiled and pulled his head down to kiss him.

They spent the night making love and it was dawn when they finally slept, wrapped in each other's arms. Maddie stirred, opening her eyes to look at Gabe. His dark lashes were on his cheeks. He was too handsome. She took in the sight of him, feeling so full of love for him that she ached. They had no future. Worse, he might be forever unhappy with her. She suspected he would never see that she had acted to save them both.

Today, he wanted her to stay in bed with him—too tempting to pass up. This was an idyll she intended to take, knowing it wouldn't happen again. Today, she had to confess the truth. Their worlds would turn topsy-turvy, and she couldn't guess what would happen to their relationship. Next week she would be home, the ranch sold, the house and contents with their new owners. She would leave Texas, but now she knew it would not be forever.

She ran her fingers over Gabe's shoulder, feeling the bulge of solid muscle, and thinking again that she loved him with all her heart.

His eyes opened, gazing into hers. He was instantly awake. "That's the best way to wake up. You in my arms, and your hands on me," he said, pulling her close to kiss her. It was a sweet good-morning kiss that swiftly changed into steamy passion. They made love for the next two hours.

The room was filled with sunshine when she lay in his arms, catching her breath. "I think it is time to get out of bed. I'll shower."

"Stop right there. I have a much better idea."

"I might as well give up on my plans."

After a half hour, she was in a huge tub of hot water, in his arms, as they sponged each other and talked.

"Shortly, we will get out of here and call the restaurant next door and have breakfast delivered. And then I will carry you back to bed."

"I would love to eat on the balcony. The view is grand and the early morning should be nice before the heat sets in."

He chuckled. "I've got news for you," he said. "It is definitely not 'early morning.' Also, you didn't want to discuss it last night and I probably should go with the flow, but I have to know… Will you spend today here with me?"

"Yes, I will," she replied.

"I'm a happy man. My wish has come true."

"You're easy to please."

"I'll show you how easy," he whispered, caressing her. "See, your reaction is enough to give me all kinds of pleasure."

"I can tell," she said, aware he was becoming aroused

again. "Before I lose my train of thought completely, don't you have to be at the ranch or let someone know where you are?"

"I'll send another text shortly. I told them yesterday that I wouldn't be in this morning."

She twisted around to look at him. "You knew how easy I would be, didn't you?"

"Of course not. But I had high hopes."

They both smiled at each other, and he leaned down to brush a kiss on her mouth.

"Maddie, this is where you belong."

He stood, pulling her up with him. They dried each other and before they'd finished, he had pulled her into his arms to make love again.

It was noon before they had food delivered. She had dressed in jeans and a blue T-shirt. Gabe wore jeans and a navy knit shirt. They sat on the balcony to eat, having a spread of both breakfast and lunch items.

She gazed at the platter of fruit, another of sandwiches, scrambled eggs, bacon, hot rolls.

"Gabe, this is as decadent as making love for hours on end. We can't possibly eat all this."

"One of us may come close. I'm starving. It's been a long time since that steak last night."

She laughed and helped herself to a bowl of fruit. "Well, the fruit looks luscious."

"I'll tell you what looks luscious," he said, gazing intently at her.

She smiled. "Don't start until we eat a bite."

"I'll try to restrain myself, but when the most beautiful blonde in Texas is sitting only a few feet away and has let me make love to her all night—"

"Will you stop!" she exclaimed. "Eat something while you can."

"Want coffee?" he asked.

"No thanks. I'll have milk. I love milk."

"So I noticed." He poured a cup of steaming coffee.

They lingered over brunch, but within the hour they were back in bed and in each other's arms.

They spent Saturday and Sunday making love. On Monday morning, while Gabe dozed, she shifted to look at him. She had put off telling him about Rebecca. But It was time to get back to the real world. This afternoon she would tell him the truth.

Later that morning as they ate breakfast inside, she toyed with her glass of orange juice. "Gabe, I need to get back to the ranch today. I've put things off so we could have this weekend, but I should return and get ready for tomorrow."

"I don't want to, but sure. We'll fly home." He pulled out his cell phone and called his pilot. "All done. I'll have you back at the ranch by four."

"Thanks," she said as her cell phone rang. She answered and heard Rebecca's high-pitched voice. She stood, glancing across the table at Gabe, who came to his feet when she did.

She motioned to her phone and left him, walking out on the balcony to talk to her daughter and then her mother.

When she said goodbye and ended the call, she turned to face Gabe. He had stepped out onto the balcony and stood by the door. His tan knit shirt fluttered slightly with the summer breeze. He was in his jeans and boots and looked relaxed, except his blue eyes were focused intently on her.

Her heart thudded, and she couldn't get her breath.

"What did you hear?" she blurted out, shocked to find him standing there.

"Sorry, Maddie, to intrude, but we've spent more than twenty-four hours in intimacy. As close as I've always felt to you, I know there's something you're hiding from me. Is there some kind of problem at home? If you're in any trouble, if you need money, you know I'll help any way I can."

She let out her breath the minute she learned that he thought she needed money. "So you didn't hear my conversation?"

"No, I didn't."

Her breathing returned to normal, but her nerves prickled. It really wouldn't have mattered whether he had heard her end of the call or not. He would never have figured out who she had spoken to.

"I'm not in any trouble. I definitely don't need money," she said, picking her words carefully. "I do need to talk to you, and I've put off doing so."

"Whenever you want," he said quietly, still studying her as if he had never seen her before.

"Let's go inside where there aren't distractions," she said, trying to compose herself.

"Sure," he said, holding the door for her. As soon as they were inside, he turned her to face him, resting both hands on her shoulders.

"Maddie, we've known each other a long time. Whatever is bothering you, you can tell me."

"I hope you feel that way after we talk. This isn't going to be easy. Let's sit, Gabe," she said, still trying to buy some time. She had decided to tell Gabe, but she hadn't given a lot of thought to how to go about it.

When she sat in a wing chair, he sat close to her on the sofa.

"Gabe, this could make a difference in our friendship."

"No, it won't. Nothing can."

"How I wish," she said. "But I don't think you'll feel that way shortly," she added, and his eyes narrowed.

Leaning forward, she locked her fingers together. "There's no easy way to do this."

Seven

Gabe sat waiting, unable to imagine what disturbed her so much He couldn't conceive of anything that would end their friendship, particularly after this weekend together, yet her apprehension showed in her brown eyes and in the slight frown that furrowed her brow. Her knuckles were white—something he had never seen on Maddie before. Through all their childhood scrapes, the arguments that last summer, he had never seen her as tense as she appeared to be this moment.

"Maddie, relax. It's me, Gabe."

"First, I want you to understand that I did what I thought was best."

"I can understand that," he said, wondering what she had done that made her think he would be so critical. He felt relaxed and curious, unable to guess what could possibly be the problem.

"I did what I thought would save us both. Promise me that you'll try to remember that," she repeated.

"This is something that concerns me?" he asked, startled. His puzzlement grew because he couldn't imagine one thing that Maddie was involved in that also concerned him.

"Yes, it does," she said, taking a deep breath.

"Say it, Maddie. We'll still be friends," he said, now anxious to have her spit it out. He was totally at a loss. How could all those phone calls concern something that involved him? He could not imagine what tie he would have to Maddie and whoever she had talked to, much less talked to in that caring, low-voiced tone.

"Gabe, I have a daughter, Rebecca. That's who I've been talking to on the phone."

Stunned, he stared at her. "A daughter? Why didn't you tell me? You said you're not married. And what does that have to do with me?" he asked. The minute the words spilled out of his mouth, he stared at her in shock. "You have a daughter and this concerns me?" he said, unable to get his breath.

Maddie's face had paled, and her hands were locked even more tightly together. She bit her lower lip.

He felt like ice. "How old is your daughter?" he asked quietly, thinking there could be only one possible, incredible, tie here.

"Rebecca is five years old now. Her birthday was in April. Gabe, Rebecca is your daughter."

Feeling as if he'd received a blow to his midsection, he lost his breath. He came to his feet, raking his hand through his hair, stunned by her news and equally shocked that Maddie had never told him.

"I have a daughter. You got pregnant that summer. Is that why you wanted me to stay so badly? Is that why you left and wouldn't talk to me?" The questions poured out. He stared at her as if he were looking at a stranger.

"To answer your questions—at first that was not why I wanted you to stay. At first, I didn't know I was pregnant. I didn't want you leaving the country when I didn't think you really needed to go."

"I have a five-year-old daughter. Five years, Maddie. This is my daughter?"

"Yes, Gabe. Rebecca is your daughter."

"Why in hell didn't you tell me?" he asked, and she flinched.

"I debated with myself for hours, days, upon end. I moved away for both our sakes."

"I don't understand how you can say that," he said, stunned, trying to think back to that summer. "Why didn't you give me some choices here? I've lost five years of her life." He paced the room without waiting for Maddie's answers. He was the father of a little girl. His child. His baby. He turned to stare at Maddie, who wiped away tears. He tried to control his anger, which simmered and threatened to erupt. Why hadn't she told him?

"Maddie, you kept the most important event of my life from me." He couldn't hold back his remarks about what she'd done. He hurt, and anger shook him beyond anything he had ever experienced. "How could you?"

"I know I kept it from you," she said, coming to her feet to stare at him. "But, back then, would you have said that her birth was the most important event of your life? Would you have wanted the responsibility of a baby? Or of marriage?"

"Hell, I don't know. If I had known I was going to be a father, I would have done the right thing. I would have married you and taken responsibility. Why didn't you give me that chance?"

"Because I thought I was saving us both. I knew you so well. Whether you wanted marriage or not, I knew you'd ask me to marry you. At that time, Gabe, you had made it clear that you were not ready for commitment. You know you weren't," she said, clenching her fists, her arms stiffly at her sides. "You would have felt duty bound to propose. I was young and inexperienced, and I would have felt duty bound to accept your proposal."

"What would have been so bad about that?" he asked.

"You weren't ready for marriage, and I wanted to leave here. I wanted college and a career and to live in a city. You didn't want to be tied down."

"It didn't mean I wouldn't have done it. Maddie, if we'd married we both might have matured and worked things out."

"Maybe, but Gabe, you left. You let me go on my way when you went yours."

He sucked in his breath as his stomach knotted. "You're right about that, but if I'd known… I could have changed. You owed it to me to tell me," he said, glaring at her, for the first time in his life angry with her. "I'm a father, Maddie. Legally, I had a right to know. Didn't you know that?"

"Yes, I knew you had rights, but I did what I thought best for the reasons I just told you," she said, her chin jutting out stubbornly.

"I think the legal reasons outweigh your immature judgment on the matter."

"Maybe in retrospect it does, but every time I thought it over, I came back to the same conclusion. You weren't ready for responsibility and marriage. I wasn't ready to give up college and the career I had dreamed about."

He felt a tight knot of anger that he was trying to curb. "Do you have a picture of her?"

"Yes, I do," she said, her voice softening. "Rebecca has your blue eyes and brown hair, but she looks like my baby pictures."

"I'm a father. That takes some getting used to," he said to no one in particular, while Maddie got her purse and pulled out her cell phone. He walked over to take the phone from her and looked at a little girl with big blue eyes. His insides clenched as he stared at the picture. "My baby. This is her." After a moment he looked up. "Can we print this out?"

"I have pictures on my laptop. I can print one of those out," Maddie replied. "I don't have it with me."

Gabe took it and felt shaken, staring at the picture of a pretty, blue-eyed little girl smiling at the camera. "She's beautiful," he said, filled with amazement to think she was his. He was a father. "She's so pretty," he said, wishing he had known her from birth.

"I think so. She's sweet, Gabe." Maddie looked at him, and he stared back, still unable to comprehend how she could have kept his baby from him. From his whole family.

"Damn, Maddie," he said quietly, still trying to hang on to his temper. "My folks are so excited over Jake's news that Caitlin is expecting a baby. They've both called me. Now I have to break the news to them that they have a grandchild they've never seen."

"Gabe, I'm sorry," Maddie stated, turning away from him to wipe her eyes. "I keep telling you that I did what I thought was best for all of us."

"Your family had to know."

"Yes, they knew. Since you had left for Nigeria, they agreed with me," she said. He knew she was crying, but all he could feel was anger for being cut out of his daughter's life for all these years.

"I didn't get to see my baby."

"Gabe, I don't think you would have felt this way about her then." She spun around to face him. "That's why I'm telling you now. You've changed. We both have. We've grown up. You told me about working with those boys. You told me how you liked the little kids you worked with. Six years ago you wouldn't have felt that way. Take an honest and long look back at that summer and how you felt about commitment then."

He clamped his mouth closed tightly, thinking back. Raking his fingers through his hair, he shook his head. "I don't know how I would have felt then if you'd told me you were pregnant. I know I would have asked you to marry me."

"I know you would have, too, whether you wanted to or not. You've always had a high sense of honor and duty. You would have pressured me to marry you. I would have married you and sacrificed my education, my legal career."

"Even so, I still think you should have let me know," he persisted, trying to absorb her shocking news. "It wasn't right, Maddie. I've lost years."

"I haven't told my family yet that you know. I told Rebecca that her father went away and didn't come back. She's little and she accepted that."

"Dammit, Maddie," he repeated. "You should have shared this with me." He looked again at the picture. "I want to meet her. I want to fly you home and meet her."

"I figured you would."

"Legally, I don't know what I can do. I'll contact my lawyer and find out."

"Gabe, don't try to take her from me. I plan to share her with you. Please don't rush into something."

"At this point, Maddie, I don't think you have a right to ask me for any favors," he snapped, aware he was giving her a harsh answer, but she had kept his baby from him all these years! "You didn't think about hurting me."

Her eyes widened, and she bit her lip, looking uncertain and worried. He couldn't take back what he said because he had meant it. He wanted to meet his daughter. "I'll tell you, I intend to be part of her life from now on."

"I expected you to. Gabe, I've thought this over these past few days. I knew telling you meant I'd have to give her up part of the time. Just remember that."

"I've given her up for five years. I would never have left the country if I'd known. We should have married and stayed a family. We both would have grown up. I'll make arrangements to fly to Florida. How soon can you get away from here for a short trip?"

"I think the earliest would be Thursday."

"No. We're going before then. You can come back. We'll take the company jet. Also, I want to tell my family. Whatever we do, Maddie, we should marry and give her my name. If you don't want to be married, we can divorce or separate, but she'll have my name and legally be my responsibility and my heir."

"Gabe, this is a huge change in our lives for both of us. Take some time to think things through."

"I don't have to think through wanting to meet her. I don't have to think through wanting her to have my name and be my legal heir."

"Even if you marry someone else later and have a family?"

He looked at the picture once more. "She's my daughter. She'll be part of my life from now on, and I'll be part of hers."

"You aren't in love with me and weren't thinking about marriage. Be careful what you do. At least, don't try to rush into an unwanted marriage. Meet her and get to know her and then we'll talk about the future."

He nodded. "We'll see. I'll think about the options and what we should do. She's with your mother now?"

"Yes. Mom keeps her while I'm away or at work. I've rarely been out of town and never away from her overnight. She loves to go to Mom's house. My grandparents love her, and she loves them. She's a joy, Gabe."

He kept staring at the picture, thinking of the years he hadn't known her. He would meet her this week. His child. "What's her full name?"

"Actually, I didn't give her a middle name. It's Rebecca Halliday."

"Then I want to give her a middle name."

Maddie nodded without saying anything.

He couldn't look at Rebecca's picture enough, and it still shocked him to know this little girl was his. He wanted to share the news with Jake, and he had to tell his family, but when he told them, he wanted to have things lined up so he could inform them what he would do and when they would see her. He didn't want his dad stepping in and trying to take charge of the situation.

Still shocked, he stared at the picture. All these years. Florida was a long way from Texas. He would have to forgive Maddie, but right now, he couldn't. He believed what she had told him—she had thought she was doing what was best for all. What she should have seen was that it hadn't been her decision alone. She should have shared this with him.

He walked to a window to stare outside without seeing any of the view. He was lost in his thoughts, running plans and possibilities through his mind.

Finally, he went to his bedroom to change and get ready to take Maddie back to her ranch.

When he returned to the front room, she waited with her things collected and ready to go.

"Maddie, I've been thinking about all of this. I postponed the flight home today by a couple of hours. I'm going to see Jake and tell him. Then he'll understand why you're changing your appointment."

"That's fine, Gabe," she replied quietly. Looking solemn and worried, she sounded subdued.

"While I'm out, I want to pick up some gifts to take to Rebecca. What does she like? I don't know anything about her! What size does she wear?"

"She's dainty, very small-boned. She wears a Toddler Five. Sometimes even a Toddler Four. She's into princess toys right now. She likes dolls, teddy bears, books, play makeup and toy jewelry. She likes to paint, and she has a small toy computer she thinks is fun. She can read. She's bright and quick. I'm taking her paints that I've already bought."

He nodded. "I'll probably call you from the toy department. I'll see you after a while." He left, knowing Maddie was hurting, but he didn't feel like offering comfort. He was adjusting to her news, still fighting his anger at her for keeping his child from him all this time.

He drove to Jake's Dallas condo. Caitlin greeted him, ushering him inside. Her auburn hair was tied behind her head. Dressed in jeans and a T-shirt, she looked as slender as ever.

"Congratulations," he said, smiling at her. "Jake told me the news."

Jake sauntered up to put his arm around her waist, and she smiled, looking up at her tall husband.

"Thanks. We're both thrilled. Thank you for the present. It will be a keepsake."

"You are welcome. I was delighted to learn I am going to be an uncle," Gabe said, wanting to focus on their news before he went to his own.

"Come in and sit," Jake said while Caitlin stepped away.

"I'll leave you two to yourselves. I'm writing letters," she said. "I know, an antiquated pastime in our electronic world."

"Caitlin, I'll talk to Jake, but you might as well join us for a few minutes and hear what I have to say. In some ways it will have an effect on all of us."

"Now I'm curious. Let's go to the front room," Jake said.

Gabe followed them past the fountain in the large entryway, into a room with leather furniture and a wall of books. As soon as Jake and Caitlin were seated on the sofa, Gabe moved to the mantel and propped his elbow against it.

"What's up?" Jake asked. "You sound as if something has happened."

"Something has. I've been seeing Maddie. She's shared some news with me today. It affects me, and both of you. If you remember, she and I broke up six years ago, and she was angry with me for leaving the country because of my job."

"I remember. Caitlin, you remember Maddie Halliday, don't you?"

Caitlin nodded. "Sure I do. We were never close friends, but we were in school together. Our families knew each other."

"Maddie and I dated before she moved away," Gabe said.

"I remember that. I had heard you left Texas because of your work and she went back to Tech. I lost touch with her and haven't seen her since."

"What's going on?" Jake asked, tilting his head. "You don't look happy, so I don't think you're going to announce an engagement."

"No. I'm happy, but my news is a shock. What I'm not happy about is that I've learned about this years later."

"So?" Jake persisted.

"Ready?" he asked, looking at his brother. "This afternoon Maddie confessed that I have a daughter. She's five years old."

"I'll be damned," Jake said, standing and placing his hands on his hips.

"Congratulations to you," Caitlin said, standing also. "I think this is something the two of you need to talk about in private. I'll leave you alone, and Jake can fill me in."

"Caitlin, you're family. I don't mind if you stay."

Shaking her head, she walked to the open door. "No. You need to talk to Jake. That's a big surprise, Gabe, to learn you have a five-year-old daughter. I'll see you before you leave," she added, closing the door behind her.

"Why didn't Maddie tell you that summer she was pregnant? Was it because she was so angry with you for leaving Texas? You always said she was getting too serious, but if she had wanted a proposal from you, I'd think she would have told you she was pregnant."

"I thought she was getting too serious, but she said when she found out she was pregnant, she knew I'd feel duty bound to propose and it would have been for the wrong reason."

She had a point. "No wonder you sounded as if the world had dropped out from under you. What are you going to do?"

"Fly to Florida later today and meet my daughter. Can we get you to change the time of your meeting with Maddie about buying the ranch?"

"Sure. I've just called Ed to make a firm offer. I think she'll accept it. We should be able to move quickly, but I can adjust my schedule so you two can go to Florida. You a dad—will wonders never cease. And before I become one. Wow."

"She should have told me. But I know she's right. I would have proposed, even though I hadn't wanted a commitment."

"Yes, I can see you doing that. It's what I would have done under those circumstances."

"She also said that she would have accepted, even though she wasn't ready for marriage. She wanted an education and a career. She wanted to leave Texas."

"That's probably true, too. Both of you were younger. There's no way you—me, either, for that matter—were as mature five or six years ago as we are now."

"I don't know how we'll work this out. I'm going to get to know my daughter. That is one thing I'm certain about."

"Why did Maddie tell you about Rebecca now?" Jake asked, his blue eyes full of curiosity.

"We've been getting close. And I told her about working with the two kids who stayed at the ranch. I told her about the kids after the storm. Because of that, she thinks I've matured and am more responsible. Maybe her conscience got to her. Jake, I've been close to Maddie all my life, but I feel like this is a betrayal. She had no right to keep my daughter from me."

"You're right, but I can see her argument, Gabe. Six years ago, you didn't want to marry. You wouldn't have done so unless you felt duty bound. You told me yourself Maddie was getting more serious than you liked and you weren't ready for commitment. You spent an hour after a rodeo, drinking beer with me and relating how much you wanted to avoid commitment."

"I suppose I did, but I still think I had a right to know."

"She should have informed you. If I were in your place, I'd be unhappy, too, Thankfully, she's told you now. At this point, I'm surprised she told you. By the end of next week, she could be back in Florida and no one here would have known one thing about your daughter."

"You're right. I should be thankful she confessed. She'll have to share Rebecca with me, and I know that will hurt her and her family. It sounds as if they adore the child. She's called Maddie often. I'd guess there have been calls I haven't known about."

"Florida is a hell of a way from Texas, but you've got your own plane, which will make it easier to fly back and forth."

"The outlook isn't good. Also, I want everything arranged and in place concerning Rebecca before I tell Mom and Dad about this."

"Oh, hell, yes. This is one time Dad would step in

and meddle in your life big-time. I don't think your income from your investments would stop him in this situation."

"No, it wouldn't."

"Don't worry. They won't hear one word from me. You can count on Caitlin to keep quiet, too, until you're ready for everyone to hear the news."

"I appreciate that. I had to tell you."

"I'm glad, but I'm not sure what I can do to help you."

"You can listen. Before I call our attorney, I want to meet Rebecca and give this more thought. I don't even know what I want at this point, except to have Rebecca in my life and see to it that Maddie shares her with me."

"Are you going to propose to Maddie?"

"I told her I want to marry, if only temporarily, to give Rebecca the Benton name and make her my heir. It'll be a name-only wedding—a business contract. Maddie is as tied to Florida and her life there as I am to Texas and my life here."

"That's what you've said. Are you sure?"

"Why do you think she's selling the ranch? She doesn't want any part of life in West Texas. She can't wait to return to Miami. From the start of this visit, she has told me she would not be coming back here. Of course, that might have had something to do with the secret she was keeping from me, because that will have to change now. She'll have to come back. But I can't see a real marriage looming. I want to marry her, to give Rebecca my name and make her legally mine. Maddie may fight that. I don't know."

"You'll work it out. You two have been close forever."

"Yeah. I should get back. Now you're an uncle, Jake."

Jake smiled. "Indeed, I am. Little Rebecca will get a bundle of relatives and in seven months, she'll have a new cousin. Rebecca Benton, the newest Benton. It's great that you have a daughter, Gabe."

Gabe shook his head. "Damn straight, but I'm still in shock." He headed for the door. In the hall, Caitlin reappeared. Jake placed his arm around her once again.

"Congratulations," Caitlin said, smiling at him. "It's wonderful news."

"Thanks," Gabe said gruffly. He walked to the door with Jake.

"Take care of yourself and let me know how it goes. I'll rearrange the appointments I have. We can work that out easily."

"Thanks, Jake. I'll keep in touch on this trip, which will be quick."

In minutes, Gabe sped away toward a local mall, where he hoped to find presents. Then he'd go to Florida and meet his daughter. His stomach fluttered at the thought.

And he still needed to decide how he would deal with Maddie. Memories of the weekend returned. He was stunned, angry right now, but earlier he had been deliriously happy with her. Had he been falling in love with her?

This weekend, he'd been happier with her than with any other woman he had ever known. In bed she was hot and wild and eager. She was the closest friend he'd ever had, except for Jake, and in some ways, Gabe was far closer to Maddie. Even when she'd been keeping this shocking secret from him, he'd been able to read her distress.

He'd already considered marrying Maddie, dreamed of it, even. But, at the same time, there were reasons he didn't want to be in love with her. Without serious compromise, any relationship would have to be a long-distance one.

Maybe he was already in love with her. Maybe he had loved Maddie for years without acknowledging his feelings. Whatever he was feeling, he wanted to marry Maddie and give Rebecca the Benton name. Would he ever get Maddie to agree?

Eight

After watching Gabe drive away from his Dallas condo, Maddie sat on the balcony with her cell phone in hand. She had to make the call and the best time to do it was while Gabe was away. Reluctantly, she dialed her mother to break the news.

Over an hour later, she'd finished her call with her mother. Maddie sighed deeply, wiping her eyes. It had been an emotional call in a day filled with raw emotions. Her mother had cried. Maddie hated that she'd had to tell her the news over the phone, but she needed to warn her family before Gabe flew her home.

She, as well as her family, adored Rebecca, who was their world. Everything they did revolved around their little girl. Maddie rubbed her forehead. After she had told Gabe, she had wondered if she had made the mistake of her life in revealing the truth to Gabe. He was hurt and angry. Her mother was hurt and angry. Her grandparents would be also.

This situation had been a mess from the beginning, but at least she felt now that she had done the right thing. No matter what upheaval this revelation caused in their lives, Rebecca deserved to know her father and Gabe deserved to know his daughter. Gabe would be good to Rebecca. Gabe was already calculating the best way to take care of his daughter. Even going so far as to make plans for a marriage that revolved totally around the benefits for Rebecca.

Which was all right, Maddie realized. If Gabe had been head over heels in love with her, it would only mean more heartache. Neither of them wanted to compromise when it came to their lifestyles.

But he wasn't in love, so it would be easier to take a practical approach to whatever they did. She just hoped Gabe never realized the extent of her love for him.

She couldn't keep from crying when she thought about this morning and his anger. She had hurt him badly, far worse than any hurts stirred up that last summer they were together. She had been the one hurt then.

What a muddle she had made of things.

Maddie went to wash her face, hoping she could control her emotions by the time Gabe returned. And continue to contain them when she got home.

Studying herself in the mirror, she gazed at her image, but could only see Gabe's eyes, earlier today, flashing fire, his hands jammed in his pockets.

She heard a car and soon Gabe entered the condo. Looking fit and full of vitality, and carrying an armload of packages, he entered the front room. Her heartbeat quickened while regret tugged at her. She hated the rift that had come between them. After the weekend they had just shared, she wanted to walk into his arms and have him hold her tightly.

He paused to meet her gaze, staring at her in a long, solemn moment before he laid his gifts on the sofa. Anger still smoldered in the depths of his eyes, and she struggled to keep back tears.

"I bought some things," he said gruffly. She looked again at the mound of packages.

"Gabe, that looks like Christmas," she said.

"I wanted some presents. I want to see if you approve," he said, and the tension eased a fraction while she walked closer to look at the array of sacks and boxes.

"I'm sure they're great."

"Maddie, I know nothing about five-year-old little girls. Come check over this stuff and tell me if it's appropriate. If you think she won't like it, I'll send it back to the store."

Maddie had to smile. "Sure." She picked up a box with a beautiful princess doll in a beaded pink dress.

"Gabe, this alone will delight her. This doll must have cost a small fortune," she said, looking at the extravagant dress that had to have been hand sewn. "This is gorgeous, and she'll be delighted with it. Rebecca takes care of her things. Probably my mother's influence. She'll treasure it." Maddie looked at the array of packages again. "Save some of those for another time."

"Okay, the doll goes with us. Put it on the other end of the sofa. The rejects we'll put on the table."

Maddie smiled again. "This is sort of overkill."

"No, it isn't. What about this?" He handed her a

large box. She opened it to see a fuzzy, incredibly soft white bear.

"Gabe, it's perfect. You have two perfect gifts. Don't give her so much she can't take it all in. Giving a little less will make what you give her more meaningful."

"You think?" he asked, frowning.

"Yes, definitely," she said, feeling amused and hurting at the same time.

"All right. I got her a little necklace. Let me include that because it's not a toy." He rummaged in a sack and pulled out a box. "It's already wrapped, so I can't get your approval on this, but I took a picture of it." He pulled out his phone and showed her.

Maddie leaned close to look at a gold heart on a chain. "It's beautiful. She'll love it."

"Oh, one more thing. I can't go without giving her a book. A book is something important. I didn't know what she had, but the clerk said this is a newer one and it's been popular. You read it on the plane and see if it's right for her. If it is, I have a gift sack and they gave me some paper."

"All right. Now this has to be all." She turned to look at Gabe, who was only inches away, and for the first time since she had broken the news, he did not seem furious with her.

He glanced down at her and then plunged back into the sack. "Don't go away."

"I thought you were going to stop with these four," she said.

He fished around and came up with a box wrapped in silver paper, bound in white ribbon, with a spray of artificial flowers and beads tied into the bow.

Startled, she looked from the gift to Gabe, who gazed back at her with a somber expression.

"Maddie, eventually, I'll get over my anger. I know you made the best decision you could at the time. I wasn't ready to settle down that summer, something I told you over and over again. I never dreamed a baby would be involved."

Her eyes stung with tears, and she wanted to reach for him, but she still felt a coolness emanating from him. "I'm glad you can see why I didn't tell you. Gabe, I worried over that decision for a very long time, all during my pregnancy and for years afterward. I'm sorry to have hurt you, but I am glad you and Rebecca will be able to know each other now."

"In the meantime, we're going to have to work together. This is an offering to make amends."

She took the box and sat to open it, taking care with the beautiful wrappings and noting the name of an expensive jewelry store.

She opened the decorative box to find a plain black box inside. Surprised again, she opened it. A delicate, filigreed gold bracelet was inside. Small diamonds sparkled in the light.

"Gabe," she said, looking up at him. "The bracelet is beautiful. This isn't just 'making amends.'"

"Yes, it is, Maddie. You had my baby. I wasn't there to give you anything then. I want you to have this."

A knot hurt her throat. She wanted to throw her arms around him and feel Gabe's strong arms holding her. She wanted their world the way it had been this past weekend. And she didn't think it would ever be that way again. Instead, she ran her fingers lightly over the delicate gold. "This is so beautiful. I don't know what to say, except thank you."

"As long as you like it."

"Of course, I like it." She looked up at him. "I wish I could make things right between us."

"We have a lot to work out," he agreed. Once again she was ensnared in his steady gaze, and the tension between them increased.

"I called Mom. She'll tell my grandparents that you know about Rebecca. She knows we're coming to Florida."

"I suppose she didn't take it well."

"No, she didn't."

"I'm sorry for that, but she was part of the decision that led us to where we are today."

Maddie nodded. She had a lump in her throat again. She looked at the boxes and her bracelet, struggling to regain her composure. "The gifts are wonderful. You didn't need to do all this. Rebecca is so easy to please."

"That's good." They faced each other, the silence growing tense once more. She ached for his arms and his cheerful optimism. A chasm had opened between them, and she worried it would never be bridged.

Then he reached for her.

"Come here," he said, pulling her close.

"Gabe," she said, unable to keep back her tears. "I'm sorry for the way everything worked out."

"Me, too. But I know the truth now, and I'll get to see my daughter grow up. Even though I don't like it, I know you did what you thought was best for all of us."

She held him tightly, wondering if he could ever truly forgive her. At least they were making a start.

"I need your forgiveness, too, for walking out that summer," he admitted, making more tears come.

"I've forgiven you, long ago. We've both moved on. We'll need our friendship to get through this, Gabe. Rebecca and I have been so close. I've spent very few nights away from her. When I came for Granddad's funeral. This trip. Other than work, and an occasional evening out when she stays with Mom, I'm always there for her."

He ran his hand over her head lightly, twisting his fingers in her hair. "I'll be there for her too, now. And for you, Maddie. You'll have my friendship. I promise." He put his fingers beneath her chin to raise her face, and she wiped her eyes hurriedly. "Sorry."

"Don't apologize. And don't cry. I'm not taking her from you. We'll work things out."

"I hope so," she said, feeling slightly better. "Gabe, I want her to meet you and get to know you a little before I tell her who you are. I'd like to introduce you as my friend, first."

He gazed into her eyes while he thought it over. "Sort of ease into the announcement. We can see how it goes, Maddie. Just don't wait too long."

"Here. I want to wear my bracelet. Put it on me please."

She handed him the featherlight bracelet and held out her wrist, watching as he bent his head to fasten the clasp. His brown hair was thick, neatly combed. She could detect the scent of his aftershave—see his thick, long lashes as he looked down to finish his task.

"There."

"Thank you. It's gorgeous, and I'll treasure it."

"I should have been there to give you a gift when you were pregnant," he said. "Did you have morning sickness or anything?"

"No. A very uneventful pregnancy and a quick delivery," she answered, looking into his blue eyes and wishing their lives were different, more compatible. She ached with love for Gabe, and she wanted a life with him, but that was impossible. "Rebecca has always been a joy. You'll see."

"We might as well get ready to go. I'll leave the other presents for Rebecca until next time," he said.

"I'm packed and ready."

"It'll take me about five minutes. I brought something for your mother and your grandparents, so take those out to go with us. You'll be able to tell because of the way they are wrapped. For better or worse, we're going to be family."

His words tore at her heart. "You're right. Our lives will be forever linked."

A muscle worked in his jaw, and he gazed back at her in silence. His anger hadn't disappeared, but it had been tempered.

She hurt deep inside. By telling the truth, she had tied her life with Gabe's forever. By telling the lie in the first place, she may have lost him forever.

"I love her with all my heart. You will, too," she said, looking into his blue eyes, still wishing things could be as easy as they'd been this weekend. Their gazes locked and tension flared.

"Stop worrying, Maddie. I told you, we'll work through this."

"I hope so, Gabe," she said softly. As she watched, his blue eyes changed. The coldness vanished and he leaned down to kiss her tenderly. She held him tightly, relishing his kiss.

"Let's get ready to go."

Shortly, Gabe returned from the bedroom and his limo driver appeared to collect the luggage and the packages.

She could feel the tension in their silence as they rode to the airport. Yes, she hurt, but if she had to do it over again, she would still tell him. She had done the right thing. She believed that now just as much as she had believed that when she'd chosen to keep Rebecca a secret. She and Gabe had both changed.

Still, she couldn't imagine how they would work out sharing Rebecca when they lived more than a thousand miles apart. Gabe had resources at his disposal—a jet, a limo—but it was a huge distance and it would complicate their lives.

An hour later, they were airborne in the largest Benton jet. Gabe had paid someone in one of the airport stores to gift wrap the toys he was taking to Rebecca. He faced Maddie, who sat close enough that their knees almost touched.

Her silky hair was tied behind her head with a scarf. She wore pale blue slacks and a matching silk blouse and high-heeled sandals. She looked cool and poised and more like herself than she had earlier today. They would spend several nights in Florida and then fly back to Texas so she could take care of the closing of the ranch house and its contents and the sale of the land to Jake.

He studied Maddie now, desire stirring in spite of the emotional roller coaster of the day. His initial anger had subsided, and other emotions were surfacing. Desire flared, hot and insistent, as if a release for all the tension that had wound between them. She was enticing. He wanted to pull her into his lap and peel away the slacks and shirt and kiss her senseless. Aboard the jet, she wouldn't allow any such thing. At her house, he wondered whether she would put him in a separate bedroom. He hadn't asked her, and no matter what conflicts still stood between them, he hoped she didn't.

She turned big brown eyes on him. "What's on your mind?"

"Guess."

She smiled at him. "Forget I asked."

"There's a bedroom on this plane. Let me show it to you."

To his surprise she began to unbuckle her seat belt. He unfastened his quickly and stood, taking her hand and leading her back to the bedroom. He closed the door and pulled her into his arms, kissing her.

Clothing was shed and then he lifted her to the bed. He loved her with an intensity that built swiftly. Kissing and caressing him, she moved over him. "Sex is a bridge over the troubles and differences between us," she said. Her brown eyes were like midnight, her lips red and swollen from his kisses.

He pulled her down to him, and, with a groan, he rolled her over so he was above her. Then he stepped away to get protection, returning to make love to her with a frantic need that he hadn't shown before.

Release brought rapture. Gabe whispered to her, murmurings she couldn't understand because of her pounding heart. "It's good between us, Maddie. So damn good," he whispered, showering her with kisses on her throat and face. "Ah, darlin', we'll get over the rough spots. Maddie, I wish I had been with you."

"Gabe, I had to let go of the 'if onlys' long ago," she said quietly, running her finger along his jaw and then over his broad shoulder.

"My bracelet is beautiful," she said, holding up her arm and looking at the faint glimmer of gold. "I may not take it off."

Gabe stretched out a long arm and turned on a small lamp on the bedside table.

"You don't need to," he said. "It's a token, Maddie."

She rose up to look down at him. "I'll always love it because you gave it to me." She leaned down to kiss him. He wrapped his arm around her to hold her close while he kissed her in return.

She shifted and settled in his arms as he turned on his back and pulled her close against him. "This is better. I don't want problems between us."

"I don't either, Gabe."

"Then we'll try to avoid them," he said lightly. "Suppose she doesn't like me?"

"I can't believe you said that," Maddie said. "You are always so filled with confidence. Since when has there ever been a female who hasn't liked you? Besides that, she's yours, Gabe. She'll be like you, so she will like you."

"I hope so. It's scary. A baby has to accept you because you're all a baby knows or has, but a five-year-old—I'm certain she has definite likes and dislikes."

"I can't believe this," Maddie said. "You make deals worth millions. Never, ever, have I seen you uncertain around a woman, and I'll bet you weren't scared around those kids who worked with you."

"That is different from this. This is my one and only daughter and I don't want to blow it."

"You've always been so self-assured it borders on arrogance. You always want to take charge of every situation, which you have done here, I might add. This nervous uneasiness is totally amazing to me."

"You're really not helping me here," he said.

"You—asking me for help—mercy," she teased, half in jest and half incredulous because it was so unlike Gabe.

He suddenly rolled her over and was on top, holding

his weight on his elbows. "You think this is funny, Maddie?" She could see the amusement in his eyes, and she wound her fingers in his hair as she laughed.

"Stop worrying. She'll love you. I love you. Rebecca will love you." She said the words lightly, aware that was the first time she had ever said that to him, assuming he would think she was still teasing him.

Instead, his eyes narrowed. "You love me, Maddie?"

She drew a deep breath while her mind raced. "Maybe it's time to be honest about everything. Yes, I love you. I always have. There hasn't been anyone else, Gabe. Not once in all those six years."

He drew a deep breath, frowning slightly, and then he leaned down to close the distance between them and kissed her, hard and long.

Her heart thudded as she kissed him in return. He hadn't said *I love you.* But now he knew. Whatever happened between them, she had bared all her secrets.

She turned slightly. "Gabe, I tried to forget you. I really did. I thought I was succeeding—until this trip."

Still, he gazed at her intently, without saying what he was thinking. "I'm glad you couldn't forget me," he said finally. Then he kissed her again, a long, steamy kiss that became making love.

Later, as he held her close, she said, "I don't want to be in bed when this plane lands. It's time to dress and go back to our seats."

He glanced at his watch. "We have a little bit of time."

"One of us is returning to her seat," Maddie said, stepping out of bed.

When she was back in her seat, she realized that their lovemaking had shattered the tension between them. She hadn't felt this lighthearted in six years. She had revealed Rebecca's identity. She had revealed the truth in her own heart. But she knew tough times still lay ahead.

It was early evening when they parked in the driveway of a small house with palms and a well-kept yard. Beds of flowers bloomed, and the porch held pots of yellow bougainvillea and green banana plants.

Gabe's palms were sweaty. "Maddie, I've ridden giant bulls that didn't make me this nervous."

She patted his arm. "Relax, Gabe. You'll see. She's a sweetheart. You don't need to wear that suit coat. It's too hot. You don't have to be formal. Rebecca will never notice. We can leave my luggage until later, but I want the brown bag, because I have presents, too."

"I'll get them." He pulled off his coat before he got out of her car. He retrieved her luggage and his gifts from the backseat. They walked around the side of the house and entered through a back door.

"Mom! Rebecca!" Maddie called.

Setting down the luggage and gifts, Gabe stood behind her, never noticing his surroundings. All he could hear was the patter of feet and all he could see was the little girl dashing into the room.

Nine

Long brown hair swung with each step. She wore sandals and a pink shirt and shorts. Gabe's heart thudded. She was beautiful, even more so than in her picture. A live doll with creamy skin, thickly lashed blue eyes. Rosy cheeks complemented her big smile. She held out her arms as she ran for Maddie, who scooped her up into a hug.

He felt a tightness in his chest as he watched them. His daughter. He loved her without even knowing her. She was precious, beautiful, his baby. It was painfully obvious that she loved Maddie, and Maddie loved her.

In that moment, he knew he had to forgive Maddie for keeping the truth from him. Maddie was levelheaded. She always had been. She told him she had done what she thought was best for both of them, and, if he was honest about the young man he'd been, he'd admit she was right. He needed to accept that, and forgive her.

After all, he had walked out on her, and he needed a bit of forgiveness himself. From now on, he was in Rebecca's life and that was all that mattered. With emotion overtaking him, he wanted to walk over and wrap both of them in his embrace, but he couldn't. Rebecca had no idea who he really was.

Rebecca's thin arms had locked around Maddie's neck, and she squeezed tightly. "I missed you," she said in a high, childish voice.

Still holding Rebecca, Maddie faced Gabe. "Rebecca, I brought my friend with me. I want you to meet him."

Rebecca looked around her mother, and Gabe gazed into huge blue eyes that were the color of his own. His heart pounded more fiercely than it ever had as Rebecca smiled and gazed at him with curiosity.

"Hi, Rebecca," he said, feeling choked, and trying to get a grip on his emotions.

Maddie turned to her mother, who was standing in the kitchen doorway. "Mom, you remember Gabe."

It was an effort to tear his gaze from Rebecca.

"It's good to see you, Mrs. Halliday," he said. He could imagine her worry about losing Rebecca to him, yet she was quiet and probably resigned to his presence in their lives.

She merely nodded, her gaze resigned and sad.

Maddie patted her mother's arm and moved toward Rebecca. "I have presents. Let's get them out." She opened the brown carry-on and pulled out a wrapped gift. "Here's something for you, sweetie."

"Let's take them in the other room and sit where we can enjoy opening them," Tracie Halliday suggested.

Picking up packages, Gabe followed the women into a small living room. It was tastefully furnished in thickly cushioned upholstered furniture, cherrywood tables gleaming with polish and area rugs. After placing all the presents on one cushioned chair, he sat in another.

"Now you can open your presents," Maddie said.

With a big smile Rebecca tore into the wrapping and pulled out paints and a huge tablet. "Thank you," she said, running to kiss Maddie, who hugged her.

"Take a present to Grandma." Maddie picked up one tied with a large pink bow and Rebecca carried it to Tracie, whose face lost a bit of its sadness as she smiled at Rebecca.

"Help me open this, Rebecca," she said, letting her granddaughter tug free the bow. Together, they tore off the silver paper, and Tracie opened a box to hold up a sparkling Waterford crystal vase. "It's beautiful, Maddie. My flowers will be pretty in this. Thank you. Isn't this pretty, Rebecca?" she asked, turning it so Rebecca could see it. Rebecca ran her tiny fingers over it.

Gabe got his present. "Rebecca, I brought you a present today, too," he said, holding out the box with the doll.

She accepted it, removing the ribbon after a struggle and then tearing off the paper. She gasped with delight. "Mommy, look!" she exclaimed, hurriedly opening the box and trying to pull the doll out of it.

"Let me help you, Rebecca," Gabe said, moving to the sofa and looking at the contents of the box. The doll was held in by wire. Gabe carefully removed it, and when he finally handed it to Rebecca, she smiled broadly.

"Thank you," she said politely, her attention returning to the doll. She gazed at it with wide-eyed wonder while she lightly touched the dress. "She's beautiful. Mommy, look. Isn't she pretty?" She carried the doll first to her mother and then to her grandmother.

"She's very pretty," her grandmother said in a flat voice.

Gabe picked up the present for Tracie and carried it to her. "Mrs. Halliday, this is for you."

Startled, she looked up and then accepted the gift cautiously. She took out a gold chain spaced with diamonds.

"It's beautiful," she said, running her forefinger over it.

"Mom, that's gorgeous."

"You didn't need to do this," she said stiffly, looking as if she couldn't decide whether to keep it or not.

"I'll be part of Rebecca's life now, and part of your life. This is a token of appreciation, for sharing her with me," he said.

Her lips thinned in a tight smile. "Thank you," she said, looking down at the necklace.

"Let me put it on you," Maddie said, taking the necklace and fastening it around her mother's neck.

"It's beautiful," Tracie said again, sounding non-committal.

Rebecca played with her new doll, and Gabe turned to pick up another present. "Rebecca, I brought something else for you," he said, holding out another box that was wrapped in pink and blue paper and tied with a pink bow.

With sparkling eyes and a big smile, Rebecca took the package and tore it open, pulling out the white teddy bear to hug it.

"So what do you say?" Maddie prompted.

"Thank you," Rebecca said instantly, holding the bear tightly. "I like him."

"I'm glad you do," Gabe said. "You'll have to think about a name for him."

"What's your name?"

"Gabriel."

"Gabrel," she declared, smiling at Gabe.

He wanted to hold her close. Instead, he had to take it slowly and let her get accustomed to him. "Now, two more things for you, Rebecca." He held out the smaller packages. She took the larger and opened it to find the book, which she ran to show her mother.

"Maybe Gabe will read it to you later, if you want," she suggested. "What do you say to him?"

"Thank you," Rebecca stated politely before running to pick up the last present. When she opened it to reveal the necklace, she held it up. "It's pretty. Thank you," she said to Gabe. "Mommy, look." Again, she hurried to show Maddie, who put it on her daughter while Rebecca stood quietly.

"I'll put all this away," Tracie said, standing to gather up the discarded ribbons and wrapping paper. Maddie stood and offered to help, and together they finished picking up and left the room.

He knew Maddie had gone so he could have time alone with Rebecca. He got down on the floor. "Let's see Gabrel," he said, pronouncing the name as Rebecca had. Instantly, she was in a world of make-believe, with the doll and the bear.

While they sat on the floor and chatted, he tried to keep some of his attention on the conversation, but his focus was on Rebecca, who played with her new doll and teddy bear and obviously loved them.

He couldn't stop looking at his daughter, wanting to watch everything she did. He played with her, talking for the teddy bear while she earnestly held the doll and made conversation.

"Do you like to play with dolls?" Gabe asked when there was a lull.

"Yes. Want to see all my princess dolls?" Rebecca asked. "I cleaned my room for Mommy, since she was coming home. I'll show you."

Gabe followed her into a hall and past one bedroom. He could hear Maddie and her mother talking in the kitchen.

"See my dolls," Rebecca said, running across a room that was obviously hers. It had white furniture, splashes of pink in the pillows, cushions and bedding. There was a large dollhouse on one side of the room. On the other was a glass cabinet filled with beautiful dolls.

Maddie entered the room. "Are you looking at all the dolls?"

"Yes. We've been playing and talking," he said, wanting to put his arm around Maddie's waist, but holding back because of Rebecca.

He spent the next half hour looking at dolls and teddy bears and talking with Rebecca while Maddie hovered in the background and occasionally entered into their conversation.

Finally, she told Gabe they would get ready to go to dinner, and he returned to the living room to wait.

When everyone joined him, they got in a limo leased from a national agency he used when away from Texas.

Rebecca was fascinated with the limo and Gabe showed her everything, letting her climb around and touch things before the driver ever started the motor.

Dinner was long and Gabe tried to charm all three females. He had known Maddie's mother all his life, but not well, and it wasn't until dessert that he wrung the first full smile from her.

It was half-past ten and Rebecca had fallen asleep when they finally dropped off Tracie and the limo drove to Maddie's house.

Gabe carried Rebecca inside while Maddie switched on lights and locked the doors.

"I can drive my car tomorrow, Gabe," Maddie said.

He shook his head. "I have a limo at my disposal. You might as well let me provide your transportation this time."

"Very well. It will complicate your schedule."

"Not so much. You can go wherever and whenever you want. Just tell the driver. My schedule is flexible."

"Thanks," she replied.

He placed Rebecca in bed carefully. She was tiny, fragile and totally fascinating to him. As Maddie slipped off the girl's shoes, Gabe looked up at the mother of his child.

"She's beautiful, Maddie," he said, wanting them to be together, to be a family. "Forgive me. I shouldn't have left you. Unfortunately, I can't take it back now. I know you did what you thought was best, too."

She hugged him, closing her eyes. "I hope you do," she said. "She likes you, Gabe." She looked down at him. "I think I can tell her tomorrow who you are."

"That scares me more than anything else that's happened in my life."

"She'll love you. You did fine with her. Let me tuck her in, and we can go in the living room to talk."

He leaned down to brush a kiss on Rebecca's forehead, watching her sleep. He walked away, stopping at the door as Maddie tucked Rebecca in and kissed her lightly. When Maddie joined him, he put his arm around her waist.

They went to the front of the house to a living room that was filled with rattan and wicker furniture, plank floors and framed watercolors of seascapes and landscapes.

"See, we're not so different when it comes to decor," Maddie said. "Want anything to drink?" she asked.

He gazed down into her big, brown eyes and wanted her with all his being. "Maddie, come here," he said, ignoring her question. He drew her close to kiss her, forgetting everything else.

After a startled moment, she wrapped her arms around his neck and clung tightly to him, kissing him in return.

He didn't know how much later it was when he picked her up to carry her to her bedroom by way of her pointed directions.

Taking time, they made love. Gabe wanted her more than he ever had. Later, as his heartbeat returned to normal, he held her close and combed her hair from her face with his fingers. "This has been one of the greatest days of my life—to see and begin to know my daughter. But I don't think I'll ever win over your mother."

"I don't know. She's just scared she'll lose Rebecca."

"I'm not taking Rebecca away from her grand-mother!"

"Mom thawed some. Thanks in part to that spectacular gold and diamond necklace. You turning on the charm at dinner helped, too. She's scared of the changes that must happen now. So am I, Gabe," Maddie said solemnly, looking at him.

He gazed down at her. "I don't have answers yet. But

I know we will work something out. I want to know my daughter. I want her in my life. I want to give her things, to do things for her."

"Let's see what we can do before we call in the attorneys."

He nodded. "That's fine with me. I want Rebecca to know me before we change any of her routines. She wouldn't want to go anywhere with me right now because I'm a stranger to her."

"You're right. It's going to mean a lot of trips to Florida for you, Gabe. I can take her back to Texas with me when I go, to help you both get to know each other."

Maddie lay in his arms with her blond hair spread over his shoulder. She looked beautiful, warm, sexy. He wanted to forget the problems between them, forget everything except her.

"Gabe, I know I said we could tell Rebecca the truth tomorrow, but I'm thinking she may need more time."

"You're right. She needs to know me better, Maddie."

"I agree. Tomorrow morning I have to go into the office until noon, then I'll take off. We can spend the afternoon and evening with her here. When we return to Texas, I'll take her with me. I want to tell her about you when the time seems right. It may be a while before I can bring it up. If it doesn't seem okay tomorrow, I won't tell her. I want her to know and like you first."

"Whenever you tell her, it'll be a shock. She'll ask me why I left. That's what you said you told her—that I left and didn't come back."

"Yes, that's what I said. When she's older, I'll explain what really happened, but I think the full truth would be confusing to a five-year-old."

"I agree. I'll keep it simple and tell her I didn't know about her birth until now or I would have come back."

"And that's the truth in the most basic manner. I think she'll accept it. I don't know whether we'll have time on this trip, but when you do have time, I made scrapbooks and videos of Rebecca that I'll show you."

"We have time now," he said, sitting up, and she had to laugh.

"It's late, Gabe."

"Not that late. Let's see the scrapbooks."

Within the hour, they sat at the kitchen table with a stack of scrapbooks. He saw that the dates covered the time from Rebecca's birth to the present. Bare chested, Gabe wore jeans and Maddie had pulled on cutoffs and a shirt.

He lost awareness of time as he pored over the pictures, running his hand over some, feeling a knot in his throat several times. It hurt to know he hadn't been a part of Rebecca's life when the pictures were taken.

Next, Maddie got out DVDs she had made, and he watched pictures and listened to Rebecca's childish voice. He pulled Maddie onto his lap and held her close, trying in some small way to get back those years and be a part of their little family.

When the DVDs ended, she turned to him, nearly slipping off his lap. "Gabe, that's all."

He kissed her, a kiss that turned into passion, but when he began to unfasten her shirt, she stopped him and shook her head. "The rest of tonight, let's sleep in separate bedrooms."

He nodded, and she stood, moving away from him. "Gabe, it's after four in the morning."

"I know," he said, standing and helping her put things away and turn off lights.

At the door of the bedroom she had given him, he kissed her again.

In minutes, he was in bed, staring into the dark and trying to sort out the depth of his feelings for Maddie. He loved her. He wanted the relationship between them to go back to the way it had been before they'd both made mistakes. He couldn't stay angry with her, and he couldn't get her out of mind. The most logical thing to do was to get married—a real marriage, not a paper marriage just to give Rebecca his name.

He thought about the past weeks and his feelings for Maddie. He was in love. Even if there had been no baby, no Rebecca, he would still love her. As for marriage, he couldn't honestly say he wasn't influenced by the reality of the situation. Under the circumstances, it was the best solution to their problems. He loved Maddie and he wanted Rebecca to be a Benton.

On the plane, Maddie had admitted she loved him. She'd even said he had been the only man in her life. Maddie had to love him with all her heart to continue to feel that strongly about him through all the years, the separation and the upheaval in their lives. They loved each other—he wanted to marry her and they would be a family.

She was so damned independent and so damned determined to live in Miami. Could *he* make a change? Maybe there was a compromise he just hadn't figured out yet.

The next day they went to Tracie's house for breakfast. She was solemn, but not as quiet as when he had first arrived. While they left Rebecca with her grandmother, he had the limo drop Maddie at her office. He would pick her up for lunch, and she would take the rest of the afternoon off work.

Gabe drove to a jewelry store. When he left, he sat in the back of the limo and looked at the six-carat diamond he had purchased for Maddie. He couldn't guess her reaction.

At lunchtime, the limo parked in front of her building, and he waited, watching her step outside into the bright sunshine.

His pulse jumped at the sight of her. She had her hair piled on top of her head, pinned and looking businesslike. Her pale blue-and-white cotton suit and blue blouse also looked conservative, part of the business world. To his satisfaction, the suit skirt was short and her long legs were gorgeous. In her high-heeled sandals and short skirt, she turned heads as she crossed the sidewalk to the limo. The driver held the door for her, and she stepped inside, looking into Gabe's eyes as she smiled and sat beside him.

"Hi," she said.

He turned in the seat, pulling her into his arms and gazing into her eyes.

He kissed her before releasing her. "I want to see Rebecca, but I also want to be alone with you. I want it all."

"For now, we'll be with Rebecca."

They had a quick lunch, then stopped for lemonade and cookies with Tracie and Rebecca before taking Rebecca back to Maddie's house. They spent the afternoon together, and Gabe had a chance to talk and play with Rebecca all afternoon and early evening before Maddie declared it was bedtime.

Gabe got to read one bedtime story to Rebecca. Holding her on his lap, he read, letting her turn the pages. She smelled sweet, and he didn't want to tell her good-night.

He hurt whenever he thought about leaving them. It was going to be hard to return to the ranch and not see them. At least he didn't have to tell them goodbye this week because they would fly back to Texas with him, but too soon they would part. He'd been mulling it over all day, but as far as he could see, there was no way he could move to Florida. His business, his family—everything was in Texas. He and Maddie had some difficult decisions ahead.

Maddie sat across from Gabe and Rebecca, watching them read. Maddie's heart twisted. Rebecca liked Gabe. She had rarely warmed to a stranger so quickly. Maddie wanted Rebecca to know the truth, but it had to be revealed carefully. She couldn't rush into it.

When Gabe finished the story, he carried Rebecca to bed and tucked her in, brushing a light kiss on her forehead before leaving her with Maddie.

Maddie smoothed Rebecca's hair from her face, gazing at her daughter, wishing she could hold her close for hours. Reluctantly, she tiptoed out of the room. She had changed to cutoffs and a T-shirt in the early afternoon and her hair was in a thick braid down her back. Gabe was relaxing on the patio by the pool.

She sat with him, and he settled her into his lap.

"You have the intercom turned on so you can hear Rebecca?"

"Yes. Usually, she's a sound sleeper," she said, looking into Gabe's blue eyes, which were filled with desire. His gaze lowered to her mouth, and her heart beat faster. As she slipped her hand across his shoulder, his arms tightened around her and he drew her close.

Her heart thudded. She wanted him. They had spent such an idyllic day together, with Gabe pouring on the charm, looking appealing and sexy as he swam and played with Rebecca.

"Maddie, marry me. I mean, really marry me. I talked about marrying in name only, so Rebecca would be my legal heir, but this is different. I love you, Maddie," he said.

She was consumed by his intensity. His declaration of love was more important at the moment than his proposal, but even while it was indelibly etched in her memory, joy and regret mingled.

"I used to dream of hearing those words from you, Gabe. I didn't, so I went out and made a life for myself without you."

He winced. "Maddie, I've done some things the wrong way, made some wrong choices. But I know what I want now. I want you and Rebecca in my life. I love you. I want us to be a family."

She couldn't catch her breath. These words were what she had dreamed of hearing—six years ago. Now her life had changed. "I love you, too, Gabe. I always have and probably always will, but life isn't that simple. I can't just marry you and—"

He placed his finger lightly on her lips to stop her arguments.

"If we can't have a real marriage now, at least marry me for the legal reasons, for Rebecca's sake. We'll work out some kind of arrangement, but it will all be easier if we are husband and wife. Marry me, Maddie. We love each other and we both love her."

Maddie's heart pounded. Everything he said made sense and would be best for Rebecca, but without full commitment and compromise from both her and Gabe it would be a sham marriage. "Gabe, I can't give up my career and my life here. I want to live in the city and enjoy everything I've worked so hard for. I'm not a rancher's wife and never will be. You won't move to Florida, will you?"

Anger flashed in his eyes. When his jaw tightened, she had her answer, the answer she had known she'd receive.

"No, I can't give up Texas, my family, my roots and everything I've dreamed about all my life. But I still want to marry you, and I want you to accept my proposal, if only for Rebecca's sake."

She slipped off his lap to walk away from him and try to clear her thoughts. She turned around to find him standing by his chair.

"You still want to marry me, even when you'll be in Texas and I'll be in Florida?"

"It's a start."

"You can't go through life with that kind of marriage."

"I don't expect to be separated from you. I want you and Rebecca to visit, and I'll come see both of you. When I can't stand living long-distance, I'll let you know, but Rebecca will have my name forever. She's a Benton and I want her to be part of the family."

Maddie's heart pounded, her mind racing over the problems and the possibilities of his proposal.

But in the end, her heart won out.

Ten

"All right, Gabe. I'll marry you," she said breathlessly, remembering all the times she had dreamed about this moment. Now that it was here, because of the circumstances, it was bittersweet.

"Ah, Maddie," he said, striding across the patio, his blue eyes filled with desire. "That's good. You'll see. You're doing what's good for her, and what's good for us. I want you in my life, Maddie, as much as I want Rebecca in my life."

His kiss left no doubt about his wanting her.

He pulled away to look down at her, combing strands of her hair away from her face. "I have something here for you," he said, withdrawing something from his pocket and handing it to her.

Surprised, she looked at the small black box in his hand. She gasped when she opened it and removed the dazzling ring.

"Gabe, this is gorgeous," she said. He took it from her and held her hand lightly while he slipped the ring on her finger. "It's magnificent. I'm stunned," she said, all her tangled emotions intensifying.

"I love you, Maddie. I should have looked at my own feelings sooner."

She met his direct gaze, wondering if they would ever work out the differences between them.

Gabe's arms circled her and, for a moment, she forgot her worries and questions as she kissed him. He carried her to bed, and they spent the night in each other's arms.

Early the next morning, Maddie was in his arms when Gabe turned to face her.

"I have a small horse, a little mare that's gentle as can be. I want to give her to Rebecca. I'll walk her around or I'll ride with Rebecca if you'd prefer."

"Sure, Gabe," she said, amused that he had so many plans so quickly. "You taught me to ride, so you can teach our daughter."

"Good. Now, on to a more vital matter—let's marry soon. If you want a big wedding, that's fine with me. Big or small, I don't care. I want it to happen. Pick a date this morning."

"Under the circumstances, I want a small wedding. Only our family and our very closest friends. That's all. Less than fifty people if we can keep it to that number."

"We can if that's what you want."

"I know you told Jake and Caitlin about Rebecca, but you still have to tell your parents."

"I haven't told my parents yet because I wanted things worked out between us first. Otherwise, that's an open invitation for my dad to step in and try to take charge."

"I hope that doesn't happen," she said, having no intention of letting his parents run her life.

"He's always concentrated on Jake. With grandkids, I think both Mom and Dad will stop interfering so much, so don't worry. I want to stay here a few more days and get to know Rebecca better. When we go back to Texas, I'd like to take her with us, but also when we go, I would like her to know I'm her father."

"I'm still waiting for the right time to tell her."

"Whether you tell her before we go or after we get there, I know you'll choose the best time. When we return to Texas, we'll stay at my place. You can make your calls there and work on getting your house ready. I'll send a cleaning crew over, Maddie, and they'll have the place in fine shape. I can do the same for a yard crew and you'll have the place ready for sale."

"Thanks, that would be wonderful and save me a lot of work," she said, relieved, yet at the same time aware it would mean she would be free to return to Florida sooner.

"If you ever decide you want to give up your career, I can easily afford for you to do that. I'll set up an account for you, so you'll have your own money."

"I have my own money," she said with amusement. "I have a good job."

"So do I, Maddie, as you know. I've been dabbling in investments for a long time now. I've done okay. Better than okay. I'm approaching billionaire status."

Surprised, she raised up on an elbow to look at him. "I knew you were wealthy, but I didn't realize *how* wealthy!"

"If you have any money you want me to invest, I'll be happy to do it. I think I told you that I handle investments for Jake and a couple of his friends. I've actually thought about expanding my business slightly."

"That is very impressive, Gabe. You're multitalented."

"So are you," he said, swinging her down to kiss her.

Then thoughts and worries were gone as she focused on Gabe.

For the next two days, Gabe gave his full attention to Rebecca.

On Thursday, Gabe showered and went to the kitchen to cook breakfast while Maddie dressed. By the time she appeared with Rebecca, he had breakfast ready and he waited, sipping a glass of cold orange juice.

In blue cotton slacks and a pale blue, cotton, sleeveless shirt, Rebecca was ready to travel. She held her white teddy bear under one arm.

"Don't you look pretty this morning," Gabe said. "We're going on a big airplane today to fly a long way to Texas. Do you have your bag packed?"

"Yes, sir," she answered. "Gabrel is going to fly, too."

"I think Gabrel will have a lot of fun on his trip," Gabe said, smiling at her.

"Rebecca," Maddie said, pulling a chair closer to Gabe's and lifting Rebecca to her lap. "See what Mr. Benton gave me," Maddie said, showing Rebecca her engagement ring.

"That's pretty," Rebecca said, touching the ring lightly. "It's beautiful," she said in her childish voice. She looked at Gabe and smiled.

"I love your Mommy, and I love you," he said.

"Rebecca, Gabe has asked me to marry him."

For the first time, Rebecca's sunny countenance disappeared. "Are you going to leave me?"

"Heavens, no!" Maddie said, hugging Rebecca. "Not at all."

"Rebecca, I want your mommy to be my wife and you to be my little girl," Gabe said, meaning it with his whole heart.

Rebecca smiled broadly, and Gabe's heart skipped a beat. He leaned closer to her. "Will you let me be your daddy?"

Big blue eyes gazed into his while he held his breath. He only took a breath once before she smiled again. "Yes," she said shyly. Relief and warmth washed over him.

"I hope so. I love you and your mommy. I want you to come to Texas and see my house."

She nodded and looked at Rebecca. "You and Mr. Benton will have a wedding."

"Yes, we will, and you'll be part of it. We have to let Grandma know this morning. We'll go tell her together."

Gabe sat patiently while Maddie broke the news to her mother and Rebecca played with her teddy bear. Mrs. Halliday seemed even more impressed with the engagement ring than Maddie had been, studying it at length and giving him a faint smile. "So, Maddie, where will you live?"

"We have things to work out, Mom," Maddie said easily. "I've told you before."

Her mother nodded, giving him another inscrutable look, but there was more triumph in it than worry, and he wondered what Maddie and her mother had discussed.

They were soon on their way to the airport. When the plane took off, Gabe enjoyed watching Rebecca's enthusiasm for the flight. She was buckled securely in her seat, but she was excited, looking out the window and commenting on everything she saw.

Gabe reached over to take Maddie's hand, holding it and smiling at her. "She's happy. I hope you are."

"I am," she said, but her words weren't convincing. The worry was back in her brown eyes, and he wondered what lay ahead for them.

In the limo on the way to Gabe's ranch, Rebecca held her teddy bear up to the window, telling him about the land around them.

Finally, they reached Gabe's mansion. Men were working on the unfinished wing. Rebecca was curious about everything she saw.

Gabe gave Rebecca a tour of the finished part of the house. When they put their bags in the bedrooms, he stepped into one and turned to Maddie. "Your bedroom will adjoin this one, which will be for Rebecca. You can start planning how you want to redecorate. When we marry, you can do this over into a room for her, and you and Rebecca can discuss what she would like to have in here."

"Gabe—" Maddie started to say, and then closed her mouth, turning away while he talked to Rebecca to tell her this would one day be her room. Maddie wondered if Gabe had assumed she would come around to what he wanted. Rebecca would visit him some, but Maddie had no intention of spending a lot of time on the ranch.

When they were together in the kitchen after putting away their suitcases, he set out steaks to thaw.

"Rebecca, I have a horse for you. She will be your very own. Do you want to go see her?"

"Yes," she said, her eyes larger than ever and wonder in her voice.

"Maddie, why don't you come with us?"

She shook her head. "I've calls to make. You take Rebecca and show her the horse," she said, watching the two of them.

Gabe swung Rebecca up on his shoulders. As they left the room, Rebecca had her fingers wound in Gabe's hair. He held the little girl carefully and both of them laughed.

As they disappeared from her view, Maddie looked down at the huge, glittering diamond on her finger. She suspected she was in for a bigger hurt than she'd had six years earlier.

She had a wedding to plan, but it would be heartbreaking because she knew their marriage was not going to be the way she had dreamed it would be. No matter how she parsed it, there didn't seem to be a way they could compromise on their lifestyles.

Gabe was ever the optimist and accustomed to getting what he wanted. This time he wouldn't be able to. She tried to focus on the list of calls she needed to make. Sell the house and furniture, finish the deal with Jake and go back to Florida. Except leaving now meant that half of her heart would be left behind in Texas.

Through the week, they stayed in Texas. Tuesday night Maddie sat in the large family room while Gabe played a game with Rebecca. He was on the floor, making her laugh as they played, her constant giggles keeping a smile on Maddie's face. Rebecca had bathed and dressed in pink pajamas covered with panda bears. Her eyes sparkled.

The hall clock chimed. "Rebecca, it's story time and then bedtime, so you two wind up that game."

In minutes, they were finished and Gabe picked up

Rebecca. "I'll carry you to your room and read one story to you. How's that?"

"Good, if you will carry Gabrel, too."

"You hold on to Gabrel and to me." Gabe swung her up onto his shoulders and she grabbed fistfuls of his hair as they left for her room. Maddie followed, watching Gabe, thinking he was everything she'd ever wanted in a man. Intelligent, generous, fun, confident—and handsome. Right now he looked great in a knit shirt and jeans. He was also a cowboy at heart and wanted his ranching life as much as she wanted the life she had built in Miami. Florida was her home, just as this Texas ranch was Gabe's home. Irreconcilable differences.

She turned down the bed and tried not to rehash the same worries she'd had since meeting Gabe on that long stretch of highway two weeks ago. She watched while Gabe and Rebecca looked through books and Rebecca selected two for him to read. He sat in a rocker and pulled her onto his lap. Rebecca settled against him, looking at the pictures as he read.

Soon she yawned, then grew still and quiet. Locks of his brown hair had fallen over Gabe's forehead. His deep voice was soft, low as he read to his daughter.

When could she tell Maddie that Gabe was her real daddy?

Sunday night, Maddie was in Gabe's arms after making love. She caressed his throat, gazing into his eyes in the faint light from a small bedside lamp.

"Gabe, the ranch and house have been sold to Jake, so that responsibility is gone. Rebecca and I leave tomorrow for Florida. You and I haven't set a wedding date. At first I wasn't sure it would even happen."

"It's going to happen. I've been thinking about our

wedding. I'd like to have a bigger one. We both have family and close friends nearby, Maddie. I want them there when I marry you." Her heart pounded with his words. He toyed with strands of her hair. "We can marry in church. Having a ceremony will mean more to Rebecca, too."

Maddie nodded, glancing at her ring that sparkled in the dim light. "A church wedding—it's becoming real. A church wedding will push the date a little farther away because it will mean more planning."

"It'll be worth it."

"Gabe, my feelings about going home haven't changed," she said, worried that he thought these days on his ranch meant she was beginning to accept life here.

"I know, but I still want to have the wedding very soon. The sooner the better."

"I agree. It will be easier to tell Rebecca that you're her real father then."

"Can you take a week for a honeymoon?"

She knew she could. She could rearrange her schedule and make arrangements with an agent to cover for her. But did she want a week alone with Gabe to become addicted to spending so much time with him? She looked into his blue eyes. "Yes, I can take a week."

"You leave tomorrow. Come back next weekend."

"You come to Florida. Then I'll fly here later."

"All right," he said, sounding reluctant. They couldn't stop time, and they couldn't change their deepest desires and feelings.

"I'll pay all expenses, Maddie. Don't argue."

"Thank you," she said, trying to imagine that their marriage would be about more than just heartache and constant goodbyes.

Her fears were compounded the next day when she stood in the airport near the walkway for the big commercial jet that she had insisted on taking home. They still had no long-term plans for when she would return to Texas, or when Gabe could come to Florida, nothing beyond the next weekend. Maddie held Rebecca's hand and the little girl held her white teddy bear.

"Come back weekend after next," Gabe urged her. "I'll fly you here in my plane. I'll come get you and Rebecca Friday night and take you home Sunday."

The offer was tempting. "Will that be our relationship—only a few days together at a time?"

"I don't know, but I'll take what I can get. I want to be with you and Rebecca."

"I'll see, Gabe," she said, her spirits sinking. Now they faced the reality of their future. It was nothing like she imagined it would be.

When he kissed her goodbye, he held her long and tight.

When Gabe let go of Maddie, he picked up Rebecca and kissed her cheek. "See the big plane you'll be on. It's even a bit bigger than the one you flew on to come here."

"Come see us," Rebecca said.

While his heart lurched, he looked into her big blue eyes. "I want to visit you more than anything, and I wish you didn't have to go home now. Someday we'll have a home together, Rebecca, because I'm marrying Mommy. When I do, I'll be your daddy."

"Can I call you Daddy?" she asked shyly, making his heart clench again. He looked into Maddie's brown eyes and then back at Rebecca.

"I would love to hear you call me Daddy. You can start right now."

She smiled and hugged him, her thin arms wrapping around his neck as they called for passengers to begin boarding. "You're my friend," Rebecca said. "My daddy when you marry Mommy."

Seeing the love between Rebecca and Gabe, and wanting her daughter to have something special as she faced her first separation from her father, Maddie said, "Gabe, this may be as good a time as any." She moved closer and placed her arm around Rebecca so they stood in a tight group.

"Rebecca, Gabe is your real daddy. He's come back to be with us," she said.

Rebecca turned wide, blue eyes on him. "You're really my daddy?" she asked.

Gabe's heart skipped a beat.

"I'm really your daddy, darlin', and I'm here now. I will always be there for you," he said, feeling a knot in his throat.

Rebecca smiled again and kissed his cheek as she hugged him. He felt as if his heart would pound out of his chest. His gaze met Maddie's, and he wrapped an arm around her. He didn't care if they were in a busy airport or what was happening around them.

"I love you both more than anything else in my life," he said in a husky voice.

"I love you," Rebecca said. "I love Mommy."

"I love you both, too," Maddie said.

"We should go, Gabe, if we're going to get this flight." Maddie stepped back and he set Rebecca on her feet. She looked down at Rebecca, who was straightening a tie on her bear.

"That was easier to do than I thought it would be."

"I'm glad. Now I can tell my parents and everyone else. Maddie, I do love you both more than anything else," he said, hurting because they were leaving.

"Gabe—" She broke off as they announced boarding for her plane.

"It's time for us to board," she said. She hugged him and kissed him briefly. He held her tightly, kissing her until she moved away. "Goodbye, Gabe. We'll talk."

He watched them disappear down the walkway. Rebecca turned to wave at him and he waved back, and hurt. It felt too much like they were walking out of his life again.

Maddie was set about living life on her own terms and he didn't think she would change. That determination was something he loved about her, but he hurt badly because he wanted them to come back. The past few days had been the best of his life. It shook him to realize that he felt that way. He was more in love with Maddie every day. And he loved Rebecca with all his heart. Love wrapped him in chains that bound his heart to theirs. He saw now why Maddie had not welcomed other men into her life. It would have been impossible, since she had truly loved him.

"Dammit," he whispered, moving to the window to watch the plane. He wanted to run and escort them off, but he knew that would solve nothing. Maybe he could give up his life and move to Florida.

He could do investments full-time. He could work on a consulting basis for Jake, but he would always want to be back in Texas. He loved Maddie and Rebecca with all his heart, but his lifeblood was this place where he was born and raised. He couldn't imagine giving it up completely. It might work for a while, but then he would want to return.

Was where he lived more important than the loves in his life? He wasn't sure. All he knew was that he already wanted to be with them.

Heartbreak tore at Maddie. She fought back tears because she didn't want to cry in front of Rebecca.

Rebecca looked out the window, holding up the white bear so he could share the view.

Maddie loved Gabe. If only she could change. If only *Gabe* could change.

But both notions were foolishness. He probably hoped the same thing. Their lifestyles were disparate, and she saw no hope of working out any satisfying solution.

She loved Gabe with all her heart. Always had and always would. Rebecca loved him now, too. He was in their lives, and they would see him, but truly living together? She couldn't fathom how it would be possible.

As time passed and they moved back into their routine lives she just hoped they could stay as close as they had been these last few days.

A week later, Maddie still missed Gabe. He had planned to fly to Florida for the weekend and then business had kept him in Texas until it was pointless for him to try to come.

To her surprise, instead of learning to live without him, as she'd done before, she missed him more with each passing day. This time was even worse in many ways than that first big separation from him six years ago. Maybe she was more in love now. Maybe they were closer, now that they had both been fully honest about their feelings and mistakes.

Rebecca missed him and asked about him and talked each day to him on the phone. Maddie's calls to him lasted for hours and added to the longing that consumed her. She planned a wedding with her fiancé much too far away from her.

She cried herself to sleep at night, and her work began to suffer. She wasn't paying attention. She had lost her drive and her focus. Even her mother seemed to be worried about her. Tracie even surprised her by asking if Maddie had ever considered going back to Texas.

Gabe flew to see them the next weekend, and they had a whirlwind visit filled with laughter and family time during the day and nights of loving that held a sense of desperation for her. She loved him and didn't want to tell him goodbye, but deep down, she couldn't help but fear their long-distance arrangement would eventually come down to them parting ways.

They would marry, and Gabe would fly back and forth until he grew tired of it. Then there would be longer and longer gaps when they wouldn't see each other.

If only she didn't feel so isolated out on the ranch… she still felt strongly that she couldn't bear to live out there.

Their wedding was planned for mid-September, but with no date set. It was not as soon as Gabe wanted, but the first they could work out a time likely to work for both of them.

She would marry him for the reasons he had been so insistent on: for Rebecca's sake, to give her the Benton name and her real daddy.

Maddie could only hope the rest would fall into place.

* * *

Gabe had a project he was involved in that took him to Chicago, and he couldn't fly to Florida. He talked to Maddie and Rebecca, but two weeks passed without seeing them, and he had a feeling he was facing what his future would be like. How long would it be until one or the other of them ended the long-distance marriage?

He missed them more than ever and each phone conversation made him long to be with them until he was completely distracted. He was to the point of worrying about handling business deals, about how long it would be before he made a colossal mistake that cost him. He could understand now why Jake had been so befuddled when he had fallen in love with Caitlin.

There had to be a way to see them more often.

Suddenly he remembered remarks that Maddie had made about cities, about her life... She liked Dallas, and both Maddie and her mother still had friends there.

Could he give up living on the ranch and move to Dallas? He thought he could, if it meant having Maddie and Rebecca in his life.

Jake would take him back into the family business at any time. And he'd been wanting to expand... It occurred to Gabe that he could live in Dallas and deal in his investments full-time.

He'd be giving up the ranch, but not Texas. Maddie would be giving up Florida, but not city life.

He had dreamed, since he was a boy, about being a cowboy, living and working on the ranch.

Could he give up that dream for the love of his life?

Eleven

On Friday, Gabe intended to fly to Florida. He had worked in the Benton offices on Thursday and he was delayed leaving, finally closing his laptop and placing it in his backpack on the way out when his phone rang. Security at the front door told him he had a visitor waiting in the lobby, though the guard didn't get the name.

Gabe said he would be right down. He closed up so he could go on to his car without returning to the office and then he took the elevator downstairs.

In the lobby, he stepped out of the elevator bank and turned the corner for the reception desk.

Maddie stood waiting. Her blond hair was tied behind her head with a red scarf and she wore red slacks and a matching shirt. His heart thudded and he walked faster. Excitement swamped him, and he couldn't overcome the urge to grab her and kiss her, to make sure she wasn't an illusion, a figment of his wishful imagination.

He pulled her into his arms and kissed away her hello. When he finally released her, he said, "I'm shocked. This is a big surprise. Did you bring Rebecca?"

"No, she's with Mom."

"If you don't want to be thoroughly kissed in such a public place, we better go outside right now."

She smiled at him, and they walked outside and around the corner of the building where he pulled her into his arms to kiss her long and leisurely. She held him tightly, kissing him in return.

"Let's go to the condo," he said gruffly, and she nodded.

"I came in a cab. I don't have any transportation. I'm with you."

"Yes, you are," he said, taking her arm and heading to his car. "This is a surprise, Maddie. I'm scheduled to fly to Florida tomorrow, so what brought this on? And without you telling me?"

"Are you complaining?" she teased.

"Hell, no," he said as he drove.

"Gabe, slow down before you get a ticket."

"I want to be alone with you."

"That's what I wanted, too. I'll fly back to Florida with you tomorrow. This is an extra day."

He didn't believe that was her whole reason, but he accepted it. He didn't care, because he wanted to make love to her and hold her in his arms. His condo had never seemed as far from his office as it did right then.

When they finally stepped inside, he shut the door and pulled her to him.

* * *

It was almost nine that night before Gabe asked her if she wanted dinner and Maddie accepted. They had made love since Gabe had closed the door behind them that afternoon. They had showered, and he wore jeans. He'd given Maddie one of his robes.

They both went to the kitchen. As she watched him move around fixing sandwiches for them, she took a deep breath, but he cut off what she was about to say.

"I'm glad you're here and that there's only the two of us, because I want to talk to you," he said, cutting thin slices from tender roast beef.

"That's why I came," she said. "To talk to you."

His eyes narrowed. He stopped what he was doing to study her. He put down his knife, wiped his hands on a towel and walked over to place his hands on her shoulders.

"I want you and Rebecca in my life full-time, Maddie. I've been thinking about our future."

"So have I. I've been miserable, Gabe."

"Maddie, I've thought it over. Now listen and hear me out. I think I've found a compromise. If I opened an investment office in Dallas and we had a Dallas home, could you tear yourself out of Florida? I know you said you had some friends and contacts, there, even a job offer. It's a big city and you've—"

"Gabe!" she cried, throwing her arms around him to hug him.

He caught her, his arms tightening around her.

"Hey!"

"That's why I'm here," she cried, feeling as if a crushing weight had lifted from her heart. "I was going to ask you if you could live in Dallas and commute to the ranch. I can get a job in Dallas."

He smiled. "I don't want to go through life with a long-distance marriage. I want you in my arms every night—or at least nearly every night. Jake asks me about every six months if I'd think about doing consulting for him. I'll have to travel some. I have some real estate investments to check on."

"I don't care, Gabe. That sounds great. I love you and Rebecca needs you," she said, the words tumbling out while she laughed and tears of joy filled her eyes.

"What about your family?"

"Rebecca will adjust. Children always do. My mom will probably come see us often. She may even move to Dallas herself."

"I have enough money I can get her a house of her own, and she can come and go when she wants. Or, we can build a big enough house that there will be room for your mother and your grandparents to come stay whenever and however long they want," he said. "Heck, they can live with us all the time! I just want us to be together, Maddie."

"That's what I want, too," she said, crying and smiling at the same time.

"You came here to ask me this same thing?" he asked.

"Yes," she cried.

"Stop crying," he said, kissing her. She held him tightly, her heart beating with joy that they had finally worked out a way to have part of their dreams and still be together. She leaned away, framing his face with her hands. "You really would work in Dallas? You can give up being a full-time cowboy?"

"I retired and moved to the ranch because I was unhappy after you left. I just didn't know why I felt so dissatisfied. I was a cowboy, but that didn't wipe out the empty feeling I had or the restlessness I couldn't shake. I just didn't recognize the depths of my feelings for you. I won't completely give up the ranch, but I don't have to live there."

"Gabe," she said, hugging him.

"We can go to the ranch some weekends. You and Rebecca can go with me. Will you do that?"

"Yes. Oh, yes. Gabe, I'm so happy," she said. "So, so happy you wanted to do this before I even asked you."

"I was going to lay out the plan this weekend. Maddie, this will make things better. If I have you and Rebecca in my life, everything else will be okay."

"I love you, Gabe."

He pulled her to him, holding her tightly as he kissed her and her heart beat wildly with joy.

He paused to look at her again. "Maddie, get a definite date set for our wedding. You might want to rethink again how big it will be. Now that we've worked this out, we may need a Texas-size wedding."

She smiled at him. "I think you're right."

Epilogue

Maddie's throat had a knot and tears of joy stung her eyes as Rebecca walked down the aisle, dropping rose petals along the way. Rebecca wore a deep blue dress that matched those of the six bridesmaids.

Maddie's white-silk strapless dress was tailored, clinging to her figure with a full cathedral train. While trumpets played, she walked down the aisle on her grandfather's arm. She paused to give her mother and grandmother roses and turned to give Gabe's mother a rose. His father smiled at her and both of Gabe's parents had made her feel welcome in their family. Then she looked into Gabe's eyes, and her heart raced with happiness.

Gabe stood tall, handsome and smiling at her, love showing in his blue eyes as her grandfather placed her hand in Gabe's warm, firm grasp. Looking handsome, Jake was Gabe's best man and Caitlin was a bridesmaid.

Maddie looked at the other groomsmen, who were Gabe's lifelong friends. And then her attention returned to her tall fiancé.

Gabe and Maddie stepped forward to repeat their vows.

Half an hour later they were introduced to the guests as Mr. and Mrs. Gabriel Benton, and then she hurried back up the aisle on Gabe's arm.

Later, at the country club reception, Maddie stood talking with her new sister-in-law. "We'll see a lot of each other," Caitlin said. "Jake and Gabe are close."

"I'm glad they are. Gabe's family has welcomed me, but then I've known all of you for most of my life."

"I'm glad for Jake and Gabe. I never had any such relationship with my half brother, Will."

"I really didn't know your brother. He was older."

"We don't keep in touch. Here comes Tony's wife, Isabelle, with Grace, Nick's wife."

"Caitlin, thank you again for the photographs you took of Rebecca and my bridal picture. I love them. You're very talented."

"Thanks. I was glad to do them. Rebecca is a doll, and she was great about posing. Jake's parents are so thrilled with her. When our baby is born, I'll have a million questions for you about baby care."

Maddie laughed. "I doubt if I'll remember. That was five years ago."

Isabelle Ryder and Grace Rafford joined them. "Maddie, you're a beautiful bride."

"Thank you," she said. "Here's who you should ask. Grace's Michael and Emily are younger than Rebecca."

"Ask me what?" Grace inquired, smiling at them.

"About babies," Caitlin said. "Maddie said it's been so long she doesn't remember."

Grace laughed, her green eyes twinkling. "I suspect it will come back to you fast enough."

"Not yet," Maddie said, smiling and glancing across the room at her handsome husband. She was ready to escape with him. He stood with close friends and his brother, but with the way he was looking at her, she guessed he wanted to get away as soon as they could, too.

"Jake, it finally happened," Nick said, grinning broadly. "You got your little brother married off." He turned to Gabe. "We never thought you'd do it and you didn't even have to be pushed into it by your dad."

"You became a dad before I did, too," Jake said.

"Which makes him the favorite with your folks," Nick added with good-natured teasing. "At least until you and Caitlin have your baby. Then you'll be the favorite son again."

"I doubt it," Jake said.

"Now that we're all married, we should take a weekend to get together and let our wives get to know each other better," Tony said. Jake agreed.

"You plan something, Tony," Nick said. "We'll have to work around football or wait until the first part of December for a fun getaway."

"Sounds good to me," Nick said.

"Y'all can plan away. Right now I have my own getaway to make. I'm going to collect my bride and see if we can't depart the premises," Gabe announced.

"Good luck," Tony said. "She'll want to stay for hours to be nice to the guests."

"He's right. Want to wager on how soon you get out of here?" Jake asked in fun, and they all laughed.

"Do what you want, I'm gone," Gabe said, walking away from them to get to Maddie. He saw her talking to his friends' wives. She was breathtakingly beautiful, but he couldn't wait to get her out of that stunning wedding gown, to take down her hair and make love to her all night.

He walked up to join the group for a few minutes. "Ladies, I'm going to steal my wife away now," he said, smiling at all of them. "If you'll excuse us. I want a dance."

They all politely agreed as he took Maddie's arm to walk toward the dance floor.

"Let's find Rebecca and our folks, tell them goodbye and get out of here," he said to her. "We can dance again on our honeymoon."

"You know we should stay for another couple of hours."

"Is that what you want to do?"

She smiled broadly. "Let's go."

They told their families goodbye, and Gabe picked up Rebecca to hold her.

"I'll miss you, Daddy," she said, smiling at him.

"I'll miss you, too, but then we'll all three go somewhere fun where you can see princesses and ride fun rides."

"I'll like that," she said.

"We'll all like it. Be a good girl," he said, kissing her cheek and setting her down.

"Bye, Tracie. Call us if you need anything," he said.

"I will," she said, smiling at him.

They left, rushing out to the waiting limo that

whisked them away before the crowd caught up with them.

As the limo drove through the Dallas streets and headed to the airport, Gabe pulled her into his arms. "I love you, Maddie. You and Rebecca are my life."

"I love you. I've always loved you," she said, wrapping her arms around him to kiss him.

When his fingers went to the buttons of her wedding dress, she caught his hands.

"Slow down, cowboy. We're still out in public."

"Not too public in here," he replied, removing a pin from her hair to let a curl fall free.

"Gabe, I have everything I could possibly dream of. We're married. We have Rebecca. Mom is moving back to Dallas. I was really surprised when my grandparents said they would move, too. I don't think they want to be away from any of us. There's only one more thing I can think of that I want," she said, twisting her fingers in her husband's thick brown hair.

"What's that? If I can give it to you, I will. I would give you the world, Maddie," he said, nuzzling her neck.

"Gabe, if we have another baby, it would be wonderful, and this time you would be…"

He kissed her hard, holding her tightly against him while desire flamed, and she kissed him in return.

They reached the airport before he released her. She straightened her dress. "Gabe, I will be a sight."

"Yes, you will. You'll turn heads everywhere you go."

"I'm so glad you have a private jet. As soon as we board the plane, I'm shedding this wedding dress."

"Fine with me. I'll unfasten the buttons."

"How kind of you," she said, smiling at him.

On the flight to their villa in the Caymans, Gabe

took her hand. As soon as they were airborne and could unbuckle their seat belts, he said, "Come here and we'll get you out of your wedding dress."

He took her to the luxurious bedroom and pulled her into his arms.

"I love you with all my heart," he said.

"Gabe, this is truly paradise. I've dreamed of this moment for too many years and then believed I had to give up my dream. But now it's come true."

"Maddie, I will try to make it up to you," he whispered as he showered kisses on her throat.

"You've already made it up to me," she replied. She framed his face with her hands. "You never answered me—do you want a baby?"

"Yes," he said. "That would be another dream come true for all of us."

"Then we'll work on getting one," she said, smiling at him.

He smiled in return as he lowered his head to kiss her.

She held him tightly, certain this was the happiest day of her life and expecting many more to come. She loved her handsome husband with all her heart, and now they would spend a lifetime together.

* * * * *

Harlequin® Desire

COMING NEXT MONTH
Available October 11, 2011

REQUEST YOUR FREE BOOKS!

2 FREE NOVELS PLUS 2 FREE GIFTS!

Harlequin Desire

ALWAYS POWERFUL, PASSIONATE AND PROVOCATIVE

YES! Please send me 2 FREE Harlequin Desire® novels and my 2 FREE gifts (gifts are worth about $10). After receiving them, if I don't wish to receive any more books, I can return the shipping statement marked "cancel." If I don't cancel, I will receive 6 brand-new novels every month and be billed just $4.30 per book in the U.S. or $4.99 per book in Canada. That's a saving of at least 14% off the cover price! It's quite a bargain! Shipping and handling is just 50¢ per book in the U.S. and 75¢ per book in Canada.* I understand that accepting the 2 free books and gifts places me under no obligation to buy anything. I can always return a shipment and cancel at any time. Even if I never buy another book, the two free books and gifts are mine to keep forever.

225/326 HDN FEF3

Name _____ (PLEASE PRINT)

Address _____ Apt. #

City _____ State/Prov. _____ Zip/Postal Code

Signature (if under 18, a parent or guardian must sign)

Mail to the **Reader Service:**
IN U.S.A.: P.O. Box 1867, Buffalo, NY 14240-1867
IN CANADA: P.O. Box 609, Fort Erie, Ontario L2A 5X3

Not valid for current subscribers to Harlequin Desire books.

Want to try two free books from another line?
Call 1-800-873-8635 or visit www.ReaderService.com.

* Terms and prices subject to change without notice. Prices do not include applicable taxes. Sales tax applicable in N.Y. Canadian residents will be charged applicable taxes. Offer not valid in Quebec. This offer is limited to one order per household. All orders subject to credit approval. Credit or debit balances in a customer's account(s) may be offset by any other outstanding balance owed by or to the customer. Please allow 4 to 6 weeks for delivery. Offer available while quantities last.

Your Privacy—The Reader Service is committed to protecting your privacy. Our Privacy Policy is available online at www.ReaderService.com or upon request from the Reader Service.

We make a portion of our mailing list available to reputable third parties that offer products we believe may interest you. If you prefer that we not exchange your name with third parties, or if you wish to clarify or modify your communication preferences, please visit us at www.ReaderService.com/consumerschoice or write to us at Reader Service Preference Service, P.O. Box 9062, Buffalo, NY 14269. Include your complete name and address.

HDES11B

*Harlequin Romantic Suspense presents the latest book
in the scorching new* KELLEY LEGACY *miniseries
from best-loved veteran series author Carla Cassidy*

*Scandal is the name of the game as the Kelley family fights
to preserve their legacy, their hearts…and their lives.*

Read on for an excerpt from the fourth title
RANCHER UNDER COVER

*Available October 2011
from Harlequin Romantic Suspense*

"**W**ould you like a drink?" Caitlin asked as she walked to the minibar in the corner of the room. She felt as if she needed to chug a beer or two for courage.

"No, thanks. I'm not much of a drinking man," he replied.

She raised an eyebrow and looked at him curiously as she poured herself a glass of wine. "A ranch hand who doesn't enjoy a drink? I think maybe that's a first."

He smiled easily. "There was a six-month period in my life when I drank too much. I pulled myself out of the bottom of a bottle a little over seven years ago and I've never looked back."

"That's admirable, to know you have a problem and then fix it."

Those broad shoulders of his moved up and down in an easy shrug. "I don't know how admirable it was, all I knew at the time was that I had a choice to make between living and dying and I decided living was definitely more appealing."

She wanted to ask him what had happened preceding that six-month period that had plunged him into the bottom of the bottle, but she didn't want to know too much about him. Personal information might produce a false sense of intimacy that she didn't need, didn't want in her life.

"Please, sit down," she said, and gestured him to the table. She had never felt so on edge, so awkward in her life.

"After you," he replied.

She was aware of his gaze intensely focused on her as she rounded the table and sat in the chair, and she wanted to tell him to stop looking at her as if she were a delectable dessert he intended to savor later.

Watch Caitlin and Rhett's sensual saga unfold amidst the shocking, ripped-from-the-headlines drama of the Kelley Legacy miniseries in

RANCHER UNDER COVER

Available October 2011 only from Harlequin Romantic Suspense, wherever books are sold.

USA TODAY bestselling author

Carol Marinelli

brings you her new romance

HEART OF THE DESERT

One searing kiss is all it takes for Georgie to know
Sheikh Prince Ibrahim is trouble....

But, trapped in the swirling sands, Georgie finally
surrenders to the brooding rebel prince—yet the
law of his land decrees that she can never
really be his....

Available October 2011.

Available only from Harlequin Presents®.

SPECIAL EDITION

Life, Love and Family

Look for
NEW YORK TIMES AND *USA TODAY*
BESTSELLING AUTHOR

KATHLEEN EAGLE

in October!

Recently released and wounded war vet
Cal Cougar is determined to start his recovery—
inside and out. There's no better place than the
Double D Ranch to begin the journey.
Cal discovers firsthand how extraordinary the
ranch really is when he meets a struggling single
mom and her very special child.

ONE BRAVE COWBOY,
available September 27 wherever books are sold!

www.Harlequin.com

SE656257KE